RED INDIAN

The Early Years

TERRY FOSS

Published by: Fossil

4 Harvard Drive

Mount Pearl, Newfoundland and Labrador

A1N 2Z7

Telephone: (709) 747 9324

Email: terryfoss@nf.sympatico.ca

Web: terryfoss.ca

ISBN 978-0-9940209-1-8

1st Edition Published March 2015

2nd Edition Published July 2015

Printed in United States

Edited by: Cathy Anstey

Cover Art: Claude Randell

Dedication

This book is dedicated to Uncle Bob (Rowsell), who instilled in me the love of books, for which I will always be grateful;

and to my grandsons, Jack and Caleb, through whose eyes I view the wonder and beauty of life.

Table of Contents

Chapter 1 ____ 2
Chapter 2 ____ 15
Chapter 3 ____ 27
Chapter 4 ____ 45
Chapter 5 ____ 55
Chapter 6 ____ 63
Chapter 7 ____ 85
Chapter 8 ____ 107
Chapter 9 ____ 134
Chapter 10 ____ 142
Chapter 11 ____ 153
Chapter 12 ____ 181
Chapter 13 ____ 210
Chapter 14 ____ 222
Chapter 15 ____ 234
Chapter 16 ____ 244
Chapter 17 ____ 254
Chapter 18 ____ 261

Part One

Before Twitter, Texting, and Facebook; before smartphones, computers, and TVs; before cars, planes, and the Newfie Bullet; before the French, and the English arrived here; a gentle and proud people populated this beautiful island of Newfoundland. This is a part of their story.

Chapter 1

1788

Shanadee

With every frantic step, her left arm slapped numbly against her side. It was acting the way it would if she had slept on it. There was feeling, not much, but some. Inside her fur mitten, the fingers of her left hand felt sticky and wet, as though they had been dipped in warm seal (monau) oil. The sharp, stinging pain in her upper arm reminded her she had been shot, somewhere just above her elbow she thought. There was no time to stop. She would have to check later, when it was safe.

Her lungs were burning. She felt she was being consumed by fire from within her heaving chest. Still, she kept running beneath the protective, deepening shadows of evening, working her way deeper and deeper into the woods. She had to get away from the pond, and the horror of what had just happened. She must get as far as she could from that terrible place. She knew she had to run to escape the White Devil. Running was her only protection against him. Father had told her that so many times.

She had heard the stories since she was little, but this was the first time she had been shot at by one of them. This was the first time she had even heard the sound of a gun. She never wanted to hear that sound ever again, but she expected she probably would.

Instinct told her he would not follow her into the woods, certainly not in the dark. He won't know this country like me, she reasoned. This is my home, not his. He's the stranger here. He's the one who doesn't belong. Still she kept running, occasionally stealing a glance over her shoulder, searching back along the way she had come for any sign she was being followed.

She knew it was a gun. She didn't know if the gun could follow her in the woods, and she had no idea how far into the woods she had to be for it not to be able to reach her. She knew it could kill her if it reached her. She continued to run.

As she zigzagged through the thickening forest, leaping over partially covered windfalls and ducking under low branches, the frightening scene refused to leave her head. It threatened to overwhelm her, and release a tidal wave of raw emotion that would surely bring her to her knees. She had to keep going. Night would come soon. It would protect her. She knew it would.

Just moments ago, she had been out on the frozen pond with her father. They had been fishing close to the shoreline, near the edge of the pond where it flowed out into a stream. The late afternoon sun had painted a pale orange glow on the snow-spotted ice. She had been playing out her weighted fishing line through the hole her father had chopped through the ice. They had already caught two good trout, and they were hoping to bag a couple more before the sun dropped all the way behind the snow-capped hills, dragging the remaining daylight with it.

Shanadee remembered being on her knees on the ice. She had been leaning over the edge of the hole, peering into the dark, shadowy water. Her right mitten lay next to her on the ice, and she was letting the baited line slip loosely between her thumb and forefinger, keeping just enough pressure to feel a strike. She remembered watching the line slide smoothly into the dark, frigid water, pulled underneath the ice by the gentle tide.

Father had been standing on the other side of the fishing-hole, between her and the nearby shoreline. He had sliced open the two trout to remove their insides and prepare them for the journey back to camp. From the corner of her eye, she had seen Father straighten up, and listen intently. He had heard something moving through the thick woods, on the other side of the pond.

"We need to go, Shanadee," he had muttered softly. The anxiety was unmistakable in his voice. It had startled her. She knew they must be in danger. He never sounded that way.

Hastily she had started to reel in her fishing line, winding it quickly and smoothly on the short alder she always used to carry it.

"No. Leave it Little One!" he had murmured urgently, staring over her shoulder at the snow covered shoreline on the other side of the pond. A thick stand of spruce outlined most of the side of the hill and ran all the way down to the edge of the ice. If there was someone over there it would be almost impossible to see them, yet worry seemed to have instantly carved new lines in his leathery, weather beaten face, she had noticed as she nervously looked up at him.

Looking into his eyes she had seen the fear, and she had let the fishing line slide through her fingers unto the ice. Suddenly she was scared. She had never seen Father afraid before. Hurriedly she had scrambled to her feet. Standing with her back to the other shoreline, she had felt something pluck at her left sleeve. At the same moment, she had seen her father stagger backward and crumple in a heap on the ice; a dark red stain spreading quickly from underneath his back in the clean white snow. She had heard the sharp crack of the gun from the other side of the pond, and she had run.

In seconds she had sprinted the short distance to the tree line. Her slight weight had easily carried her over the hard crusted snow. She had left her snowshoes back there on the sled, even though she had known she would probably need them later. Anyway the snow had a light crust on it here and it was easy to run over the top of it. Running was something she was good at, and this time it just might have saved her life.

The second shot had thudded into the trunk of a thick spruce tree, kicking up a spray of bark and wood splinters that had showered down over her head as she raced past. Instinctively she had ducked lower, changed direction yet again, and raced into the shelter of a stand of evergreen. The forest had protectively closed around her, and she was gone.

Finally she stopped running. She thought that by now she had run far enough away from the pond to be safe. Exhausted, she dropped to her knees in the snow next to a tall fir tree. Its large branches formed a sheltering canopy overhead. Resting her back against its thick trunk, she tiredly closed her eyes. Her heaving lungs created a cloud of steam that swirled around her and hung there like a thin curtain, in the still evening air. Gradually her breathing returned to normal and her racing heart slowed, no longer threatening to leap out of her aching chest. Leaning her head back against the hard trunk, she opened her eyes and stared up through the overhanging canopy of fir boughs that were laden down with a covering of fresh snow. Through the gaps between the branches she could see the sky was turning dark. Nervously she looked back the way she had come, anxiously scanning the path her footprints had made in the snow. Holding her breath she listened intently. There was no sound. No one was following her. At least, no one she could see or hear.

Looking around her, she could find no sign of life anywhere. Other than her footprints, the snow was undisturbed. She was all alone out here. There was no one to help her. If she was going to make it through this, she was going to have to do it on her own. She couldn't remember a time in her life that she had felt so lonely and afraid.

"Why?" she moaned aloud. "Why did they do that? Oh Father! I should have stayed to help you!"

Deep in her heart, she knew with a certainty that if she had not run, she would have died there on the ice too. They would have shot her down just like him. Still, she felt like she had abandoned him. She had left him at the time when he had needed her most. He had always been there for her, and now she had let him down.

But what could I have done, her anguished mind whispered? There was a gun.

She had spent most of her time with him, since she had made her first steps. He had taught her everything she needed to know to survive in this harsh land. She remembered how his face would always turn serious when he talked about the White Man (Buggishaman).

"Run, Little One," he would say. "Run if you see the Buggishaman." "Don't let him catch you, don't ever let him catch you. You are Beothuk and the Buggishaman hates the Beothuk."

Now she finally understood what he had meant all those times.

Maybe I should go back, she thought. Maybe I can still do something.

Twisting to push herself to her knees, she unintentionally put weight on her left arm. The searing pain that lanced up her arm into her shoulder made her gasp in agony. She slumped back against the tree, closed her eyes, and waited for the throbbing to stop. It felt as though someone had taken a live coal from the fire and placed it inside her arm. She hadn't noticed it when she was running. She had been too busy getting away.

Gingerly she opened and closed her sticky fingers inside the wet mitten. A soft moan escaped through her clenched lips. She tried to bend her arm and the numbing pain forced her to bite into her bottom lip. The salty taste of blood filled her mouth. Fighting the waves of pain she slowly bent her arm all the way up at the elbow. I guess it's not broken or I wouldn't be able to do that, she thought with some relief.

Reaching around with her right hand, her probing fingers found the ragged tear at the back of her left sleeve. The red leather was dark, black almost, where it had been soaked with blood. The edges of the torn leather had been burned by the passing bullet. Through the jagged hole in the caribou skin she could see the dark bloody slash on the side of her upper arm. It didn't look very deep; but it was still seeping blood. She had been lucky; the bullet had barely grazed her.

Gripping the tip of the wet mitten, she tugged it off her hand. Its mate was somewhere back there on the ice, next to the fishing-hole. Carefully she unwound the bindings that attached the sleeve to her cloak, and pulled the sticky arm cover from her injured arm. The fur inside the sleeve was soaked with blood, staining it a dark red. Mother will have to make a new one, she thought grimly, and new mittens as well. She probably won't be too happy about that!

With the tip of her knife, she pricked several bulging myrrh bubbles on the trunk of the fir tree. Using her finger she smeared the pungent, oozing liquid, on the open gash. It felt cool to the touch and she spread a thick coating of it on her arm. That should keep it from bleeding anymore, she thought.

Next she sliced a narrow strip from the bottom of her cloak, and wound it around the open cut on her arm. She tied a knot and pulled it tight by gripping one end with her teeth, and the other by her right hand. Then she wriggled her torn arm cover back over the bandage and laced it up.

"That should do for now", she said. Talking aloud helped her feel a little less alone; maybe a little less scared too.

Looking up through the trees she noticed daylight had begun to fade from the sky. Night was fast approaching, and soon it would get dark. She had stayed here too long already. It was time to get moving again.

While she had been working on her arm the sun had pulled all the warmth from the air, dragging it along as it slid from sight behind the distant hills. Shanadee shivered as the cold wind rustled around the tree, shaking the snow from its laden branches. Her heavy fur coat had been left back at the pond as well. She remembered taking it off and tossing it on the sled as her father was cutting the fishing-hole.

It really was time to get on the move, or she was going to freeze to death in this cold.

"I need to get back to camp and get some help. There's no point going back to the pond. It's too late for that now, and anyway it would be too dangerous," she said. "It'll be dark soon and I only have one good arm. I'll get my uncle. He'll know what to do."

Wearily she pushed herself to her feet. She had no heavy coat, one mitten, and no snowshoes. This was going to be a cold night. Taking one last look back along the trail of her footprints, she turned and began the long, cold walk back to the camp. The band members had only just finished setting it up this week. It was on the banks of the river, so she knew if she followed the ice she would find it, even in the dark. Her mother and two brothers were waiting there, with the other two families of their little band.

"How am I going to be able to tell Mother about Father?" she said. "She will be so sad. What will we do without him? What will I do without him? I miss him so much."

"Why did we stop at that pond?" she cried to the silent woods.

Trudging wearily through the trees, the tears finally began to flow, leaving dark streaks of red ochre (odemet) coursing down her face, like jagged lines of war paint. The knot in her stomach clenched her insides in a claw-like grip, and the nausea pushed the bitter taste of bile up into the back of her throat. Determinedly, she forced it back down. She stopped walking and leaned against a tree. With her right sleeve she wiped the cold sweat from her brow. Dropping to her knees at the base of the tree she scooped a handful of snow, and wiped it over her flushed face. The cold shock of it on her hot skin made her feel a little better.

Still, no matter how hard she squeezed her eyes tight she could not make the pictures go away. The horror of seeing her father crumbling to the ice was burned into her memory.

Another wave of nausea washed over her, and she released it into the snow.

Wiping her mouth with the back of her hand, she pushed herself to her feet once more and started walking again. It became an automatic thing, driven by instinct, each step bringing her closer to home.

Nothing in her twelve years of life could have come close to preparing her for this. She had heard the stories of the Buggishaman, lots of times; but she never expected her first encounter to be this way.

"This is not how it is supposed to be," she mumbled. "We are not animals, to be hunted. We are people just like they are!"

"I need Father," she sobbed. "We all do."

There were places, here in the woods, where the crust of snow wouldn't even carry her light weight. More and more she found herself breaking through and sinking in the snow up to her knees. Without her snowshoes, she knew she couldn't keep walking like this. Each time she fell, her arm throbbed with new pain, and she knew it would only get worse. Cautiously she worked her way back to the river's edge.

Hidden behind the thick trunk of a large tree that leaned out over the river bank, she carefully checked downriver for movement. He was still out there somewhere, with that gun. She studied every inch of the shoreline back to where the river bent out of sight. Seeing no movement, she slid down the bank and moved out onto the ice. She put her head down and started forward again, following the shoreline back to the camp. The bitterly cold wind almost forced her back into the shelter of the woods, but she determinedly plodded on towards home.

That day a tiny seed of hatred was sown deep in her young innocent heart. It would become a weed that would grow, and send its bitter shoots throughout her being, finding root deep in her soul until it controlled her life and ultimately shaped her destiny. There would be no mercy for a people that would hunt her tribe like wild animals.

Out on her left she noticed movement from the corner of her eye. She stopped and stared into the shadowy woods but could see nothing. Her hand protectively closed around the handle of her knife. Small protection she knew but it was all she had. She started to walk again keeping an eye on the woods and she saw it emerge from the shadows. It was a large wolf (moisamadrook). His dark grey fur blended with the shadowy woods, making him almost invisible. She slipped the knife from its sheath and held it at her side. Anxiously she scanned the woods for others. She couldn't see any, but that didn't mean they weren't there. She had no idea what to do next. There was nowhere to run, and she couldn't outrun it anyway.

She had been taught to not make eye contact with the moisamadrook, but there was something different about this one. Its long gray tail dragged on the ice and its ears were standing forward on its head. Both were signs that it was not in an aggressive mood.

The moisamadrook slowly walked to the edge of the ice and sat watching her. Shanadee looked directly into its eyes and suddenly recognition made her cry aloud, "Father!"

Her heart jumped in her chest. She knew it was her father's spirit. She saw it in its eyes. It made her so happy that he had chosen to show himself this way. He always promised her that he would never leave her, no matter what.

Aloud to the night, she said, "I see you Father. I will find the man who did this to you; and I will kill him. Revenge will be good."

Chapter 2

1788

George

Standing in the small, one room tilt, surrounded by a swirling cloud of steam and smoke, George wrapped the tattered dish cloth around the wire handle and slid the boiling kettle from the blackened sapling that suspended it over the open fire. Drawing in a deep breath through his nose, he savored the delightful smell of the rich dark tea as it poured from the kettle into the waiting tin mug. It was one of his favorite times of day. He loved to sit in the rickety old wooden rocker he had built, sipping a cup of strong tea, and letting time slip away as he watched the single wax candle slowly melt beneath its tiny, flickering flame. The dancing shadows it threw around the room were in constant motion, as the flame was drawn in every direction by swirling drafts surging through the seams in the wooden slat walls. It was a soothing and peaceful place; a place where he could relax and remember. It wasn't much, nothing more than a shack really, but he had built it, and it was his.

The smell of the hot tea and the gentle motion of the rocker relaxed him and gave him time to reflect on the life he was carving out for himself in this wild new colony.

It would be six years ago this spring, he and his younger brother Tom had left their family home in England, found their way to the docks, and there booked passage on a sailing ship bound for the New World. Their young minds had been stirred by misrepresented and greatly exaggerated tales of adventure and opportunity in that far away land somewhere on the other side of the ocean. Tom, with his restless spirit and unquenchable lust for adventure, had convinced him that this would be a trip of a lifetime; a chance to be among the first to experience the new frontier and share in the bountiful riches of the new land, was how he had put it. Although he'd had strong misgivings about the whole thing, George had finally agreed to accompany his brother, to keep him out of trouble more than anything. He had to admit there had been something enticing about being among the first to explore a new land. He was not sure he still felt that way, but there was something nice about being alone out here, he thought, as he gently blew on the surface of the hot tea to cool it before taking the first sip.

Somehow tonight, the dancing shadows reminded him of the wildly heaving seas that he had watched night after night from the constantly moving deck of the ship that brought them here. He shifted uneasily in the rocker. Those were not memories he enjoyed, in fact he'd just as soon forget them. That unending ocean voyage had very nearly been his undoing. After the first hour or so he had quickly discovered that he was not going to be able to spend any time below deck. In the enclosed space the motion of the ship had made him violently ill. Scrambling up the ladder, he had crawled out on the windswept deck and that was where he stayed. He had spent most of the voyage lying on the deck thinking what a stupid decision he had made and regretting the day he had ever stepped off dry land.

The memory was so vivid he absent mindedly ran his tongue over his lips as if he could still taste the salt that had been left by the flying spray.

The sea sickness had been so completely disabling, he would have stepped off onto any rock in the middle of the ocean, rather than spend another day on that rolling ship. So when the barren rocky shores of Newfoundland finally materialized out of the thick, swirling fog, he would have jumped over the rail into the chilly Atlantic and swam ashore if he hadn`t been so weak.

Their passage had been paid back in England before they got to board the ship, so when the anchor dropped over the side George was already leaning on the rail ready to scramble down the rope ladder into the waiting boat that would take them to the beach. For his brother's sake, Tom had made sure they were on the first boat to go ashore, so as soon as they were given the go ahead Tom slung the bag with their few possessions over his shoulder and followed his brother down the ladder.

The sickness had passed once he stepped ashore, at least enough that he no longer wanted to die. He was weak from eating nothing on the trip, and it took the best part of the week for him to regain any strength at all.

Tom had looked after him back then. In fact, if it hadn`t been for his brother, he knew he wouldn't have made it through that horrible time. Tom told him he'd lost so much weight he could have passed him on the street for a stranger if he didn't take a close look. Since then he often said to Tom, "If the only way off this God forsaken rock is by boat, then I'll never be leaving this place. I don't intend to ever go through that nightmare again; not as long as I live."

For the first couple of years, they worked at whatever they could find around St. John`s harbor. Work wasn't always plentiful, but it got them by and paid for their room at the boarding house down by the waterfront. As much as possible George avoided jobs that required him to go aboard the sailing ships, but eventually work took him there. He made it through it with Tom's quiet coaxing. That was the funny thing. No one would ever believe Tom had a sensitive side, and Tom would never want anyone to know it either, but it was there, carefully buried beneath that rough exterior.

Around the docks Tom was the loud one, the one commanding attention with his big stories and grand schemes. He had a way of drawing people to him, and he usually found a way to get what he wanted. Then, as always seemed to be the case, Tom`s wandering spirit had kicked in. He could never settle in one place for very long because there was always the next big score waiting out there for him.

Lifting the warm mug to his lips, George took the first mouthful, swished it around and let it flow down the back of his throat. The hot liquid warmed him, and he leaned his head back until it rested against the high back of the rocker, closed his eyes and savored the feeling. His mind wandered back to Tom, and he smiled as he remembered lying in the dark, in their little boarding house room, listening to Tom's constant chatter from the top bunk.

"Hey George, I heard some fellers talking about the salmon fishery on the rivers further up the coast. They say there's lots of money in it and you can make a good living at it. The best part is that you are on your own. Nobody looking over your shoulder all the time, now that would be alright wouldn't it, George? I could get used to that!"

"Them fellers was sayin' the river is swarming with fish and they say there's no body to bother you up there, 'cept a few scared Indians. They're no problem. You just got to show them who's in charge, that's all."

"How do these fellers know all that, Tom?"

"Well, this feller what I was talkin' to had been talkin' to a feller what just come down for supplies. He was on that boat that we was unloading yesterday. Remember them barrels of salmon we pulled up out of the hold? They come from up there."

"Where's this to?"

"Like I said, it's up the coast on a big river."

"That's far, isn't it?"

"Couple hundred miles or so, I s'pose."

"What do we know about salmon fishing, Tom by'?"

"We'll learn, George. It can't be all that hard, by'. Anyway it's got to be a whole lot better than this stuff we're at. Pretty much anything would be better than this I'm thinkin!"

"When are you ever going to stop wandering all over the place, Tom?"

"When I'm rich, George, when I'm rich," Tom had laughed. "So what do you think? Are we gona give it a try or what?"

"I don't know. You had better find out more about it before we goes traipsing all over the country. I'm certainly not going anywhere by boat, you know that for sure."

"I knew that!" laughed Tom. "It'd take something to get you back in one of those things my son, wouldn't it now!"

Tom had kept the pressure up for a week or so and finally George had just given in. They pulled together the necessary supplies and early one morning they had left St. John's and set out overland for the Exploits area. That had been a great trip. They had finally got to explore country that had not been visited by many before them. Camping out in the woods like that had been their first exposure to the wild country. George loved it. He knew this was where he was supposed to be. After all, this was why they had come over here in the first place.

That trip had taken them more than a month through some of the toughest country they had ever encountered, but they had eventually reached the place where the Exploits River emptied into the sea. A small but busy settlement had sprung up there. Asking around on the wharf, they were told Old Man Peyton would buy all the salmon they could catch. It looked like he controlled the salmon fishery on the Exploits River.

George was startled out of his reverie by a loud banging on the wooden door that rattled it in its frame. He flinched, as the hot tea spilled and began seeping through his trouser leg. Pinching the wet material with his fingers, he lifted it away from the bare skin and set the mug aside.

"George, George, you in there?" shouted a familiar voice.

"Yes Tom, I'm in here," George replied through the closed door. "You scared the livin' daylights out of me, by'. Come on in. The kettle is boiled."

"You got to come out here and see what I got, first," Tom shouted back.

George released the wet trouser leg and pushed out of the rocker. He lifted his heavy woolen coat down from the peg beside the door, swung the door wide, and stepped out into the cold crisp air of the late evening.

Shoving his arms into the sleeves of his coat as he walked, he said, "What's all the racket about, Tom?"

"I got another one George", said Tom, grinning proudly.

"Another what?" asked George, although he figured he already knew what the answer was going to be.

"Another one of them thieving Red Indians, by'. I got something for my trouble this time too," said Tom, proudly pointing to the sled that was standing alongside of George's pile of loosely stacked firewood.

"Where did you get that, Tom?"

"I shot a Indian up at the head of the pond. There was two of them, but the young 'n got away. Ran like the devil, she did. They was ice fishing. There`s a couple of nice trout there on the sled. We can have them for supper," smiled Tom, as he continued walking toward the sled.

Following him through the light snow, George launched into a conversation he'd had with Tom many times before.

"Why are you shooting Indians Tom? They are not animals, you know."

"They are just a bunch of thieves, George. They'd steal the eyes right out of your head if you weren't looking," Tom muttered, as he picked up the two trout from the sled.

"Tom Rowsell, you are just bringing trouble to my door. Don't you think they will track you here?"

"Na, she was just a kid. Anyway, I know I hit her, 'cause I saw blood on her trail. She probably didn't get too far at all. If it hadn't been getting dark I would have found her for sure. She won't be any trouble to anyone."

"This has got to stop, Tom. You know I don't want any part of this killing."

"You're getting soft George," Tom needled him.

"Not really Tom. How many times do I have to tell you? I don't have no quarrel with the Indians. They are only trying to survive, you know. If they take a salmon or two out of my traps, well that's OK. After all, they was here long before we was. We are the ones who are trapping and fishing on their land. So tell me, who's taking from who, Tom?"

"It ain't nobody's land, George, not theirs and not ours! It's just land, that's all. Here, take these will you," he said, holding out the two trout. "Let's go in and have them for supper now, and stop this arguing. I got to get back down the river tonight before it gets too late."

Later, after Tom had left, George moved back to the rocker. He sat there, amidst the lingering smell of fried fish, and got to thinking about the Indians again. Tom's view was shared by many of the other settlers around these parts. He knew that for sure. Problem was, this kind of thinking, more often than not, resulted in violent encounters with the Beothuk. Most always, the Red Indians came out the losers. They didn't stand much of a chance with their home made arrows and spears against the settlers guns.

Sometimes though, the Indians were their own worst enemies. It seemed their way was to share everything, and not to have individual ownership of anything. So when this attitude was extended to the English property, they were seen and treated as thieves.

Although he wasn't happy with the idea of them taking his scarce fishing gear, he never took issue with them taking the occasional salmon from his traps. Because of this, he seemed to have established a workable relationship with the local band. They did not fear him and seemed to have a healthy respect for him. Often, they would run out on his weir while he was there, spear a fish, and run back into the woods. Some of them would raise the fish in the air and call "Gorge Rosel." It seemed to be their way of thanking him. This may have been why they never did any real damage to his fishing gear. It just goes to show, we can live together if we try, thought George.

One thing was for sure, they were a very nervous lot. He couldn`t remember a time when they had shown themselves when somebody else was with him. He only ever saw them when he was alone.

He chuckled softly as his mind drifted back to the incident last summer.

Early that morning he had gone down to the river to see how the salmon were running. When he got to the riverbank, he discovered the small boat he used to travel the river was not where he had left it. As he looked upriver a commotion on the other side caught his attention. Three Beothuk men were jumping up and down and waving their arms in the air to get his attention. Laughing loudly, and slapping each other on the back like children, they waved at him and pointed to the boat that was pulled up on the shore at their feet. They seemed to think they had played a great prank on him. Understanding what they were up to, George had smiled at them and waved in acknowledgement.

Later in the day, after he found his way across the river and retrieved his boat, he found a brace of rabbits they had left for him lying there in the bottom of the boat.

This land has plenty of wildlife and it is big enough for all of us, thought George. The attitude of his brother and the others toward the Beothuk was born out of a selfish mentality of exploitation. It could never come to any good end, certainly not for the Red Indians.

Shaking his head in bewilderment, George wondered what would become of it all as he bent and blew out the flickering flame of the candle. Before lying down on his bunk, George stood there in the dark for a little while, just listening to the peaceful silence of the night. This is a great place to be, he thought. We made the right decision to come to this island.

He had almost drifted off to sleep when he heard a scraping on the outside of the wall next to his bunk. Must be a fox or something, he thought sleepily, as he pulled the blanket a little tighter around him.

Chapter 3

1788

Manddilleeitt

Manddilleeitt had spent most of the day chewing strips of dried caribou skin, softening the tough leather so that she could form it into moccasins for her family. Over the past couple of days she had finished a pair for each of the two boys, and now she was getting ready to sew a pair for her oldest child, Shanadee.

This wasn't as easy as it used to be. Time had not been kind to Manddilleeitt. What with so many missing teeth and the stiffening of her fingers in the last year or so, making moccasins was getting harder and harder. She remembered a time when she would have been able to finish all three in the same day. Getting older was not a lot of fun, but then she had her family and that was all that really mattered to her.

She glanced over at the two boys who were sitting on the other side of the fire that smoldered in the center of the wigwam. They were staining their finished moccasins with a mixture of dark red odemet and monau fat. Manddilleeitt smiled as she watched Timmwall as he showed his little two year old brother the proper way to spread the thick mixture. He was acting more and more like his father every day. Things needed to be done right, or there was not a lot of point in doing them. If you're going to do the job, you've got to do it right, Nanolute would say, smiling disarmingly.

Little Jaywritt was more interested in tasting the mixture than learning how to spread it on the moccasins. Timmwall repeatedly pulled his brothers dripping fingers from his mouth. "You can't eat that stuff. It'll make you sick," he said patiently for the third time.

"Listen to your brother, Jaywritt, "said Manddilleeitt as she put the pieces of caribou skin aside and pushed some more wood in the open fire pit. She placed her two hands flat on the smooth dirt floor, awkwardly pushed herself to her knees and stood up with a soft groan. The dull ache in her side was giving her more trouble than usual today. With one hand pressing against the sore spot on her lower back, she shuffled to the thick black bear skin that hung over the door opening, and pulled it aside. She had been sitting cross-legged on the hard floor so long her legs had gone to sleep. The blood was returning to them, and her skin felt like it was being stung by a hive of angry bees. She ground her few remaining teeth together against the pain.

"Where are those two," she wondered aloud, "It's getting dark and it's time for them to be back." Shanadee and her father were always out wandering around the countryside, doing something or other. Sometimes she wondered if Nanolute was treating their daughter too much like a son. Already he had taught her how to use both the long bow and the short bow (hathemay). She practiced with them so much; none of the boys in the tribe could match her shooting. She should be spending more time working around the camp, like the other girls, thought Manddilleeitt. Nanolute was turning her into a hunter like himself, and that wasn't what she wanted for her only daughter, well, not *just* that. She supposed she might even be a little jealous of all the time they were spending together. Shanadee had always been a poppa's girl, ever since she could crawl. A slow smile crinkled the corners of her mouth as she realized how silly her thoughts were.

"Crazy old woman thoughts," she muttered under her breath.

Shaking her head, she absentmindedly rubbed her back as she stooped and peered out the open flap of the wigwam. The wigwam had been built at the back of a small clearing, nestled up against a stand of tall spruce and fir, with the door facing the lake. Nanolute always built it that way. He loved to hear the sound of the water when he was going to sleep at night and the first thing he wanted to see when he looked out the door in the morning was the lake.

Scanning the snow covered lake she noticed motion in the distance. Was it a single person moving along the shoreline, on the far side of the lake? The late evening shadows played havoc with her vision, and she could not be sure. A worried frown creased her brow. If the figure across the lake was a Buggishaman, they had to be ready to abandon the wigwams and run. Too many of the tribe had already been slaughtered by their guns because they didn't run. Nanolute had been careful to drill that into his family. Run from the Buggishaman and you will live to enjoy another day, he'd always say. If you let him catch you he will kill you.

She couldn't be sure, but she could only make out one person, so it couldn't be Nanolute and Shanadee. I wonder why they are so late, she thought uneasily.

Over her shoulder, she murmured to the two boys, "Someone is coming. Gather what you can. We are going to run and hide in the woods."

"Why do we have to run mother?" asked Jaywritt, looking up from his partially dyed moccasin. "What about Shanadee and father? How will they find us?"

Full of questions as usual, Manddilleeitt thought, as she hastily replied, "We will leave signs and they will track us. Hurry now! I must warn the others. It may be the Buggishaman."

Timmwall slipped the new moccasins on his brother's feet and handed him his coat. "Put that on. It's cold outside, and we don't know how long we will be out in the snow."

"What does the Buggishaman look like Timmwall?" he asked, as he struggled to get the heavy fur coat over his head. "Will he hurt us?"

"Stand still, little brother," said Timmwall, as he pulled the coat into place and helped Jaywritt push his arms through the sleeves. "We have to hurry. There isn't much time."

Manddilleeitt picked up the little birch bark drum that was hanging near the door. Standing just outside the open door, she tapped out five quick sharp sounds; the prearranged danger signal between the three families. In the quiet, late evening air, the sound would easily carry to the other two wigwams a little further up the lake. She knew they would have heard it, and would already be preparing to run. They would all meet later tomorrow, at the spot they had picked deeper in the woods, away from the river.

Across the lake, in the fading light, she could just make out the distant figure stop and turn. It was too dark to tell, but it almost looked as though it waved in her direction. The fading light was playing tricks on her eyes she knew. She quickly turned back into the wigwam and helped the boys roll their sleeping furs into a tight bundle. Throwing the bundle over her shoulder, she grabbed a bag of dried meat and another of dried egg yolks from the floor. She reached out and slipped her hand over Jaywritt's little hand and stepped through the door into the night. Timmwall followed close behind. Over his shoulder he carried his hathemay and a sheath of arrows. Without his father and Shanadee here, protection of the family fell on his young shoulders. At nine that might be a daunting task, thought Manddilleeitt, although she couldn't help but be proud of the way he was handling this.

Taking one last look back over Timmwall's shoulders, Manddilleeitt felt the cold chill of fear crawl over her crooked back. If that was a Buggishaman out there on the ice, she wanted her family to be far from here. She turned away from the lake and was hurriedly leading the boys into the woods, when Timmwall, who was protecting the rear of the family, whispered urgently, "wait!"

"What is it son?" Manddilleeitt replied softly, freezing in her tracks.

"Listen! Do you hear that, Mother?"

Faintly in the darkness Manddilleeitt heard the call. "Mother, it's me."

With a gasp she dropped her load. "Here, take your brother," she said to Timmwall.

Pushing her back pain aside, she began to awkwardly run towards the frozen lake, toward the familiar voice of her daughter. Even at that distance, she had picked up something in her daughter's anxious tone that scared her. Her mind raced ahead of her, rushing to a place she did not want it to go. Where was Nanolute? Something had happened. Why was Shanadee alone?

"Are you alright," she yelled as she slid down the snow bank onto the ice. Scrambling to her feet she began to run again.

They met on the ice in the fading light, which was still enough for her to see the answer she was dreading in her daughter's watery eyes. Falling to her knees on the crusted surface of the snow covered ice; she began to wail the song of mourning as she slowly rocked back and forth. Shanadee wrapped her good arm around her mother and held her tight, fresh tears flowing freely into her mother's dark, oily hair.

Realizing they were no longer alone, Shanadee lifted her head. Through her tear filled eyes she saw that the other families had gathered around them and were standing quietly in a protective circle. Jaywritt was clinging to Timmwall's side, sobbing loudly. He really had no idea what was going on, but seeing his sister and mother crying was enough to tell him something bad had happened. Timmwall had an arm around his shoulder, trying to be the big brother, but she noticed the tear streaks on his face as well. She met his eyes and saw understanding there.

Beeroute, her father's brother, stepped forward and gently lifted Manddilleeitt to her feet.

"Come back to the wigwam", he said. "It's warm inside. We must attend to Shanadee." He had noticed the jagged rip and the wet stain on her sleeve. "She is freezing out here."

Manddilleeitt brushed his hands aside and turned to her daughter in alarm. "Are you hurt?" she asked, with a mother's concern in her voice.

Shanadee nodded and turned so her mother could see the torn sleeve. She was shivering uncontrollably. Now that she had stopped walking she felt the bitter cold wind biting through her thin cloak. Suddenly she felt she couldn't take another step. The determination that had kept her plodding through the night was fading and she just wanted to sit down on the ice and go to sleep.

Manddilleeitt gasped and wrapped her arms protectively around her daughter. "Is it bad? Can you move your arm? Let's get back to the wigwam and take a look," she blurted out, without stopping to take a breath. "You must be freezing," she said as she grabbed a blanket someone handed her, and wrapped it around her shivering daughter.

"It's ok Mother," replied Shanadee tiredly. "It's not deep."

Grabbing her other arm, Manddilleeitt hustled her towards their wigwam, rattling out commands to those around her, as she hurried Shanadee across the ice.

"Stoke the fire."

"Boil some water."

"Get me some myrrh. Quick"

By the time they reached the wigwam, those who had run ahead already had a pot of water hanging on a pole over the crackling fire. The first thing Shanadee noticed was the warmth inside. She closed her eyes and let it wrap around her like a blanket. She was safe now. Her long ordeal was over. She was home. It was going to be ok.

Manddilleeitt quickly guided her to the far side of the wigwam, away from the door. Then she pulled away the blanket and proceeded to strip her daughter to the waist. Manddilleeitt then carefully examined her daughter's body, looking for her injuries.

"It's only my arm," Shanadee protested, "everything else is ok. I'm cold."

"Keep that door flap closed," Manddilleeitt said without looking up.

Once she was satisfied that there were no other marks, Manddilleeitt wrapped the blanket around her shivering daughter again and carefully cut away the blood stained cloth, covering Shanadee's injured arm. She gently peeled the sodden cloth away from the gash, allowing the strong aroma of the myrrh to swirl around them. "Good," she mumbled. "You did a good job, Shanadee. If we keep this clean it should heal."

Using hot water from the simmering pot, she carefully cleaned the skin around the bloody gash. Then she mixed some ground dandelion leaves with myrrh and applied a liberal coat over the opening where the Buggishaman's bullet had grazed Shanadee's arm. Manddilleeitt then wound a clean piece of cloth around the injured arm and tied the ends. She smiled at her daughter and hugged her tightly. "It will be ok," she whispered in her ear.

Shanadee stayed there, locked in the safety of her mother's tight embrace. This was what had kept her going all night, out there alone on the ice. Somewhere outside in the night she heard the lonely howl of a moisamadrook and she smiled.

Someone handed her a clean tunic and she slipped it on. As if on a prearranged signal, everyone found a seat on the ground around the fire. Each set of eyes turned expectantly to Shanadee.

Looking around the wigwam at all the familiar faces Shanadee felt safe again. Her eyes were heavy and all she wanted to do right now was sleep, but she knew they wanted to know what had happened and where her father was. She just wanted everyone to go and leave her alone, but she knew this had to be done. Reluctantly, she took a deep breath and began to talk, hesitantly at first, but stronger as she continued.

"Father and I were fishing on *Pond with Little Island*. Father chopped a hole through the ice. We caught two big trout; one each. Then Father heard someone coming through the woods on the other side of the pond. He said we had to go and to leave everything. Before we had a chance to leave he was shot. I ran like he taught me."

"How did you get shot?" asked Manddilleeitt, a solitary tear slowly trickling down her face, following one of the deep lines that marked her weathered cheeks.

Looking up into her mother's troubled eyes Shanadee replied softly, "The shot that hit Father struck me first."

Manddilleeitt looked at her daughter sadly. She knew she would always carry the scar on her arm, a constant reminder of the shot that killed her father. She wished she could somehow remove the scar.

Jaywritt left his brother's side and lay on the ground next to his sister with his head in her lap. Shanadee gently scratched his head as she talked. The warm fire was making him sleepy and his heavy eyelids slowly closed.

"Did you see the Buggishaman?" asked Beeroute.

"No. I never looked back. I just ran."

"You were very lucky, Shanadee," said Beeroute, "you did the right thing". Murmurs of agreement rustled around the room.

Sitting next to the warm fire, surrounded by her family and tribe members, Shanadee no longer felt cold and afraid. This was a good place; a safe place. She wished Father was here too. Then everything would be perfect.

Beeroute looked at the other two men sitting next to him. Without speaking they nodded in agreement.

Jumping to his feet, Beeroute announced, "We will track him."

The three men slipped outside and walked across the clearing to the edge of the frozen lake.

Looking up at the clear night sky, Beeroute said to the others, "I will go alone. You stay and watch the camp."

"Do you think he will come here"?

"Probably not, but you never know with the Buggishaman. He killed for no reason at the pond so he may be hunting us. You need to keep a good watch and be ready."

"We will. You go and find your brother's killer."

"Will you kill him?" asked his wife's brother, Jeddilledt.

"No. I will find out who he is first. Killing will come later. It is Shanadee's right to avenge my brother. She has earned it."

"Is she old enough"?

"Yes," replied Beeroute, "she is old enough and we will help her."

The others nodded in agreement.

"Your brother was a good man," said Jeddilledt, "He will be missed."

The three trudged back to the wigwam in silence. Inside, Beeroute selected his brother's long hathemay and a quiver of arrows from the shelf overhead. He pulled on a heavy fur coat and caribou skin mittens.

"I will find the Buggishaman," he said to Shanadee and her mother, as he stooped and shuffled out of the tent, letting the stiff bear skin slap the post as it fell back in place behind him.

Beeroute picked up the snowshoes that were leaning against the side of the wigwam and without looking back, he headed out onto the frozen lake, following Shanadee's trail.

Even by the dim light of the moon, it wasn't hard to follow her tracks and Beeroute ran in the open places. He knew he needed to make good time if he were to catch this one.

He found Nanolute on the blood stained ice. His sled, boots and jacket were gone, and the rabbit foot charm he always wore around his neck was missing. Not satisfied with just a killing the Buggishaman had robbed him of anything of any value. One of Shanadee's mittens lay frozen onto the ice next to the fishing-hole.

Frost had already laid claim to his brother's body. He could feel no warmth in him. His spirit had left long ago.

Kneeling on the ice by his side Beeroute grew angry.

Beeroute was not only taller than his little brother by at least two hands but he was also much heavier. He had always been, not just the older brother, but the bigger brother. He had been twelve years old when Nanolute was born, and he instantly took on the role of his little brother's protector. Through the years he had been there when his brother needed him, until now. Now he had failed him. It had to be made right.

"I will come back for you little brother," said Beeroute softly. He pushed to his feet, turned, and began to run down the center of the tracks left by the sled. The Buggishaman had stayed on the snow crusted, ice, making it much easier to follow him.

At the far end of the pond, the tracks left the ice and followed a beaten trail along the riverbank. Beeroute knew this area well. The fisherman they called Gorge had a tilt on the river nearby. He was a friendly man, who had never done any harm to the Indians as far as he knew.

Beeroute began to run again, following the sled tracks up to the wood pile stacked near the dark tilt. There were two sets of man tracks in the snow leading up to the door. The sled was nowhere to be seen.

Beeroute leaned against Gorge's overturned boat. It was the same one that he and his brother had taken across the river last summer as a practical joke on Gorge. It had been Nanolute's idea. That was the way he was, always teasing someone or playing a joke on them. Beeroute hadn't been sure it was such a good idea at the time but he had gone along with it, and it did turn out ok in the end. Gorge had been a good sport about it. Remembering made him smile.

There were no lights or sound coming from inside the tilt. It appeared his brother's killer had stopped here for a while before continuing on.

Beeroute soundlessly crept up to the tilt and put his ear to the rough wooden wall. Through the gaps in the boards, he could hear faint snoring inside. So, it was someone else who had killed Nanolute. That is good, he thought. I would not have wanted it to have been Gorge.

Turning to leave, he accidently scraped the hathemay that was hanging on his shoulder against the wall of the tilt. He froze, listening for movement inside. Hearing nothing, he backed quietly away from the tilt until he reached the woodpile. There he found the trail left by the sled, and the Buggishaman who pulled it. Moving quickly along the trail and reading the markings in the snow, he could tell that he wasn't far behind his prey. He quickened his pace a little.

When he reached the place where the river flowed into the next pond, he saw that the sled tracks had returned to the ice. He stopped at the edge of the pond and stared intently out across the ice while his breathing settled down. In the distance he could see movement. Overhead the clouds covering the moon scuttled away, and in the faint moonlight he could make out the outline of a man and a sled, silhouetted against the white, snowy background. He knew it had to be his brother's killer. His heart began to pound faster as the anger rose within him. He felt his hand curl around the wooden handle of the knife at his side.

Bending low, he raced along the shoreline. The riverbank was low here and the trees grew right up to the water's edge, giving him plenty of good cover. He needed to get out ahead of the Buggishaman, so that he could get a close look at him.

Within minutes, he had closed the gap to where it was no longer safe to stay in the open without risking being seen. Beeroute slipped into the woods, and ran as silently as he could, but it was much slower going. The snow was not crusted like on the ice and he broke through the surface more times than not. He was breathing heavily as he pushed through the deeper sections.

When he thought he had gotten far enough ahead of the Buggishaman he angled back to the river that flowed out of the end of the pond. He knew the Buggishaman would keep following the river trail because it was easier going with the sled. Careful not to make any footprints where they could be seen, he searched along the trail until he found a good hiding spot, just off the path behind a short spruce. He scooped out the snow behind the tree and made a small hole to lie in. Satisfied that he couldn't be seen there, he placed his hathemay on the snow within easy reach and lay on the frozen ground. Ignoring the cold, he covered himself with snow and waited.

The sound of cold snow crunching under the taunt strings of snowshoes announced the arrival of the Buggishaman before Beeroute could see him in the darkness. Moments later he appeared out of the night, trudging down the trail toward Beeroute's hiding place. He was pulling Nanolute's sled with a rope that he had looped over his shoulder. In his free hand he carried a long gun; the gun that must have killed

Nanolute. Beeroute had never been this close to a gun before, but he had seen what they could do. He had seen how they spat fire and how easily they could kill a man. He knew the gun could kill from a great distance; much further than you could shoot an arrow.

He had been returning from a caribou hunt with four men of the tribe. It was several years ago, but he could still see the pictures clearly in his head. He had been much younger then. They had been walking along the trail that led up the back side of a low hill overlooking their camp. Suddenly, the air was filled with loud bangs coming from the direction of the camp. They had dropped their loads of meat and raced to the top of the hill. Below them was a scene of panic with people running in all directions. The Buggishaman had surrounded the camp and were shooting from all four sides. In horror they watched their families fall under the fire from the guns. Shouting at those below they had fired arrows at the shooters but they were too far away. The arrows did not even reach their mark but the return fire from the guns did. Two of them were shot before they could turn and run for cover. At least some of the tribe had been able to reach the woods and escape when the Buggishaman had turned their attention on the hunters, he thought. At least they had been able to help some of them.

He held his breath and lay completely motionless, hoping he had covered himself with enough snow. The bright, round moon overhead was not helping him. Hopefully the spruce bush was big enough to hide the disturbed snow. The muscles in his arms and neck were coiled with tension. The sweat on his forehead was cold and he had held his breath so long his chest was tight with pain.

As the Buggishaman passed close to Beeroute's hiding place, he saw his face in the moonlight. He also saw the rabbit foot, dangling from the rope that tied his coat at the waist.

Carefully Beeroute let the air escape from his aching chest as he watched the sled move away down the path. He knew who this man was! He fished salmon (wasemook) on the river like Gorge did. He had killed Indians before, probably many. He was one of the ones they told stories about around the campfires. The tribe had been warned to stay away from him.

Beeroute's fingers tightened on the hathemay in his hand. He could easily surprise him and kill him now. Then it would be done. Problem was, he had promised to let Shanadee avenge her father's death. That was her right. He should not take that away from her. Flexing his fingers on the hathemay he reluctantly watched his brother's killer walk away into the night. He knew there would be another time, and this was not the last time he would see this Buggishaman.

Chapter 4
1788
NANOLUTE

Beeroute did not take the river trail back. He was in a hurry to reach the camp to get help in bringing his brother home. Strapping on his snowshoes, he took one last, lingering look down the trail where his brother's killer had disappeared, turned and headed across country, in a direct line to the camp. He walked out of the woods, into the clearing behind his wigwam, just before the sun appeared over the trees.

He selected a clean deerskin blanket and strapped it on his sled along with his snowshoes. Before leaving, he upended the sled and applied a liberal coat of monau fat to the wooden runners. The fat would help it slide over the ice more easily, especially with the heavier load on the return trip. Then, pulling it behind him, he walked out on the ice and made his way down the lake to Manddilleeitt's wigwam.

As he approached the clearing, Jeddilledt and his friend stepped out from behind the trees where they had been keeping watch.

"How did the night go"? Beeroute asked as he climbed up the low bank.

"It's been quiet here," Jeddilledt replied softly. "Everyone is asleep now."

"Get your snowshoes," said Beeroute. "We'll go and get my brother."

"We are ready," said Jeddilledt. "Did you find the Buggishaman"?

"Yes. I tracked him down river. It was the one called Tom. The one they say killed many Beothuk."

"Did you kill him"?

"No. I could have done it, but I left him for Shanadee."

"She is young."

"It is her right. I will be with her. It will be done when the time is right."

"Let's go."

Silently, the two men fell in behind the sled as Beeroute set out, dragging it across the ice.

Beeroute set a fast pace and the sun hadn't cleared the trees by much by the time they reached the pond where Nanolute lay. A lone gray moisamadrook sat on the ice nearby, as if guarding the inert body. Jeddilledt notched an arrow to his bow and walked out ahead of the other two.

As he approached, the moisamadrook stood to its feet, and moved off towards the little island in the center of the pond. It sat and watched them from there.

Beeroute dropped to his knees and inspected his brother's partially frozen body. He could find no sign that the moisamadrook had touched his brother, despite the blood on the ice underneath him. Thoughtfully he raised his head and looked at the animal across the ice. He stared into those dark eyes for a moment and whispered, "Go in peace brother."

Carefully they rolled Nanolute's stiffened body unto the blanket. Beeroute wrapped the deerskin tightly around his brother and together they lifted him onto the sled and tied him securely to the frame. Beeroute pulled Shanadee's mitten from the ice and tucked it into the blanket with his brother.

No words were exchanged by the three men while they worked. They seemed to understand what was expected of them, and just did it. These were the fluid actions of men accustomed to working together.

When they finished, Beeroute stood, and looked up at the cloudy sky. He tentatively sniffed the air. "Weather's coming," he said, as he went to the front of the sled, swung the rope over his shoulder, and began to pull. Jeddilledt pushed from behind to start the sled moving, and the three men began the walk back, following their own earlier tracks. Beeroute glanced over at the island. The moisamadrook was no longer there.

Before they reached the end of the pond, dark, angry clouds swirled across the sky, quickly obscuring the morning sun. A biting cold wind raced down from the surrounding hills, wildly swaying the leafless trees at the side of the pond. Light snow began to fall and was caught by the rushing wind and whipped around the three men. It was as though the gods were unleashing their anger on the forlorn scene below.

Bending low, the three leaned into the wind, and pushed on towards the camp.

A single, snow covered figure stood on the snow bank that outlined the edge of the lake, and watched the procession approach across the ice. The smoke rising through the roof of the wigwam behind her was instantly yanked away by the angry, howling wind. The blanket that she had loosely wrapped around her shoulders fluttered and flapped wildly in the swirling gusts. She stood there motionless as if she had become part of the cold lonely landscape.

With the help of the other two men, Beeroute pulled the sled up onto the snow bank, and stopped in front of his brother's wife. She dropped to her knees at the side of the sled, reached down, brushed the snow away, and gently lifted the deer skin from her husband's face. With tears in her eyes, she bent down, gently cupped his frozen face in her hands and kissed his forehead.

"Take him to our wigwam," she said to Beeroute. "We must prepare him for his journey."

The three men unlaced the bindings, removed the body from the sled, and carried it inside. They placed it on the dirt floor near the fire. All three quietly left, and returned to their own wigwams, leaving the little family to their mourning.

Shanadee moved their furs to the back of the wigwam away from the fire. All that day, while the storm hurled itself at the sides of the wigwam, she sat on the furs listening to the fury of the wind and snow outside and tried her best to comfort her two brothers. It was up to her to look after them until her mother's mourning was finished. She was the eldest. She wished she didn't have to do this. She needed to mourn Father as well, but it was what had to be done.

The room was filled with moaning and the desperate sobs of their mother, who sat rocking back and forth on the floor, next to the still body of their father. Shanadee's heart felt as though it had been pierced through with many arrows. The gnawing pain and overwhelming emptiness was too much to bear. Father was gone! She would never again feel his strong hands covering hers, as he showed her how to draw and release her long hathemay. No more would she smell his familiar scent or hear his spontaneous laughter that had always made her feel safe, letting her know he was nearby, and all was well.

She tried her best to comfort the two boys but her heart was heavy with sadness and she could not hold back her tears for long. Timmwall sat quietly by her side with his head resting on his knees. Little Jaywritt was too young to understand. He crawled up onto her lap and wrapped his arms around her neck.

"What's the matter sister?" he asked looking into her teary eyes. "Why is mother crying so much? Why isn't Father moving? Why doesn't he stop her?"

Whispering quietly to him, Shanadee tried to explain. "She is sad because Father is going on a long trip to the land of Gosset."

"Are we going too?"

"No little brother. He can only go alone."

"When will he come back?"

"That's why mother is sad. He can't come back from there."

"Then why is he going?"

"Because the evil Buggishaman killed him," Shanadee whispered bitterly.

"You mean like when you kill rabbits?"

"Yes."

Jaywritt snuggled into her chest and was quiet for a while. She wrapped her arms around him and held him tight. He is so young and innocent she thought.

"Did the Buggishaman want to eat him?" asked Jaywritt, without raising his head.

"No Jaywritt. Why did you ask that?"

"You and Father only kill rabbits for food."

"It wasn't for food," Shanadee whispered pressing her cheek against the top of his head.

"Then why?"

"They are evil people, little brother. They want to kill us because they hate us. You must never let them see you. Always run and hide." Shanadee's last words were whispered through clenched teeth. She felt the anger welling up in her chest again.

Sensing her anger, Jaywritt snuggled closer to his sister. He played with the rope belt of her tunic, twisting it around and around his fingers. "Why didn't you stop him, sister? You are a good hunter. Father always says so."

Shanadee's anger was washed away with fresh tears. Her feelings of guilt and confusion returned. "I wish I could have, Jaywritt, but he had a gun," she replied with a heavy heart.

"What's a gun?"

"It's a terrible thing. It's a long stick that makes a loud noise and spits fire. It throws things that will go through you and make a hole in you. It can do this from far away, much further than we can shoot arrows. He would have killed me too if I didn't run, like Father taught me."

"I'm glad he didn't kill you, sister," he said wrapping his arms around her neck and squeezing as hard as he could.

"I'm glad too," she smiled and kissed his cheek.

"What does a Buggishaman look like?"

"I didn't see this one Jaywritt, but I've seen them before. They are just like us except they have white faces and they wear different clothes. You will know if you see one.

Jaywritt crawled down from her lap and lay on the furs. He closed his eyes and was soon fast asleep.

Timmwall, who had sat quietly through the exchange between his brother and sister, now whispered to Shanadee, "Will you kill the Buggishaman someday?"

"I think so," she replied.

Later that evening the storm eased up and as it began to grow dark, the flap was drawn back from the door, admitting the rest of the women of the band into the wigwam. After some vigorous stamping and brushing to get all the snow off, each in turn hugged Manddilleeitt. Then, as Shanadee and the boys watched from the back of the wigwam, they set about preparing Nanolute for his trip across the river of death, to Gosset, the country of the dead.

First they removed his remaining clothing and washed his entire body. Next they applied a fresh coating of odemet mixed with monau fat until his whole body was colored red. While the others were applying the coating, Manddilleeitt knelt on the floor by his head and oiled and combed his long black hair. Then she tenderly wove a single braid in it, and fastened a shiny black crow's feather at the crown.

Together, the women carefully lifted Nanolute's body unto sheets of birch bark that had been sewn together in large squares. Wrapping it tightly, they sewed the loose ends snugly against the body.

The men were then called inside, and they lifted the wrapped body and carried it out of the wigwam. Once they were outside they lifted Nanolute to their shoulders, and set off towards the edge of camp leading a procession of the entire band.

Because the storm had been so strong they had not been able to finish constructing the small wooden enclosure that was normally built to hold the body until the snow melted, and the frozen ground could be dug, to provide a final resting place. Instead they carried his body to an empty wigwam where he would stay until they could construct the burial enclosure in the next few days. Beeroute placed Nanolute's hathemay, several arrows, a knife, and a drinking flask, next to the body as protection on the journey down the river. Lastly he retrieved, from the bag hung at his side, a carving of a canoe (tapaithook), he had worked on all day. It would help carry his brother's spirit safely to the other side of the river. Placing it next to Nanolute's head, he then followed the others outside and securely fastened the door.

The small group stood in front of the wigwam softly chanting death songs that celebrated Nanolute's life. Finally, Beeroute held up his hand silencing the group. Facing the door, he said in a loud voice," Go in peace little brother. Have a safe journey. We will see you again someday."

While they had been placing her father in the wigwam, Shanadee had been watching the grey moisamadrook. It was sitting in the snow at the edge of the woods, just outside the circle of tribe members. As if responding to some signal, it rose to its feet when Beeroute finished speaking, swung its head towards Shanadee, turned and walked into the darkness.

There was something final in that. She knew she was now on her own. She also knew deep in her heart that she would someday avenge her father's killing. She would be patient. It would come. She knew it would and she would be happy when it did.

Chapter 5
1789
TOM

It was 5:30 in the morning, still dark enough to see some of the brighter stars hanging in the black canopy overhead, yet with just a hint of the coming day. Tom turned away from the single window in his small shack and finished dressing, which consisted of hauling on his rubber boots and slapping his cap on his unruly head of hair.

By the time he stepped outside, letting the cabin door slam shut behind him, night was in full retreat, relentlessly pursued by the strengthening light of the advancing day. The water in the little cove stirred and rippled, as if brushed by the nights passing. Tom could feel a trace of subtle warmth in the air. It looks like it will be a fine day he thought as he followed the narrow footpath that zigzagged around some of the larger boulders on its way down to his wharf. At least he considered it a wharf. George thought it was just a mess of half-finished ballast beds connected by a few wooden rails that still had most of the bark left on them. You're taking your life in your hands walking on that,

George would say. But then never mind George, he's afraid of the water anyway. He's not about to go out on any wharf any time soon.

Tom had started to build the wharf last year. Someday he would finish it. Of course someday was his plan with most things. Seldom did anyone ever see a completed project of Tom Rowsells'. Tom was easily bored, always jumping to something more interesting, than what he was currently working on. If it's good enough to use, then it's good enough, was Tom's motto.

From the head of the partially completed wharf, you could see around the sandy point where the river poured into the sea: where the fresh water mysteriously became salt. He always wondered about that. How you could taste the water at the end of the river and it was fresh, yet soon as it got in the cove it tasted salty. Strange!

He had picked this spot because it was close to the river. The less he had to row the better. It would still take him a couple of hours rowing and walking to get up river to his salmon weir. It wasn't that he was afraid of work; it was the unnecessary work he had no time for. "It's going to be another long day," he grumbled aloud to himself. "I've got to find something better than this salmon fishing to do."

George had passed through a couple of days ago with a big load of gear on his back. He still avoided boats on the open water and only used one when he had to on the river. After all this time, thought Tom, I guess he's never going to get over it now. He smiled as he thought of his brother's irrational fear of boats.

George had set up his camp and salmon weir another mile or so further up the Exploits River from where Tom had his camp. Tom had first pick as usual, and George had deferred to him as always. George is too easy, thought Tom, things never change with him!

Tom tossed his gear in and pushed the little flat bottom river boat off from the wharf into the early morning mist. The thick, grey mist lay heavily on the water, rising a foot or so above the surface, so that Tom was sitting above it as the boat pushed its way through. As he rowed, he watched it swirl around behind the little boat, quickly filling in the spaces where his passing had disturbed the quiet air. The only sounds were the rhythmic dipping and lifting of the oars, followed by the dripping of water as they were swung out to dip once more. He kept time to these sounds by humming an old tune under his breath.

Underneath his seat lay his flintlock, with the long barrel stretching out between his feet, pointing toward the back of the boat. His powder horn hung loosely around his neck across the front of his chest. That way he made sure the powder stayed dry, and was in easy reach if needed. The gun was loaded and ready to fire, as it always was. Tom's habit was never to venture inland without being prepared to shoot Red Indians, and you couldn't do that if your gun wasn't loaded. If they happened to show themselves he wanted to be ready. Thing was they seemed to be keeping more under cover nowadays. Probably knows I'm around, thought Tom. That's why I haven't been able to get one for a while now.

Cutting through the still water of the shallow cove, his mind drifted back over the last couple of years. According to his reckoning he had brought down seventeen of them; a couple a more that he couldn't confirm, like that young girl up near George's tilt, last winter. Chances were she crawled away into the woods somewhere and died from the gunshot wounds. He was almost certain he had hit her. The idea that he had probably got two of them with the one shot brought a smile to his face. That was some shooting! It would be nice to get three more though, just to have a nice round number. That would be something to brag about to the boys when he went in to St. John's later in the summer.

His mind turned to his brother again. He just couldn't figure George out. What was he thinking anyway? He had turned into a regular Indian lover. He even had a good relationship with that Great Lake lot. That'll be the death of him one of these days, when they turn on him. For turn on him they someday will. I just know it. Then he will understand what kind of animals they really are. It'll be too late then!

Problem was George was actually feeding them. That was like feeding a stray dog for sure. You'll never get rid of it. No way! Well, George is a big boy and he can take care of himself I suppose! He don't need me looking after him anymore. Still, I hope nothing happens to him.

I wonder if the salmon are running yet. The spring runoff seems to be pretty much done. That should mean the level of the river will be back to normal by now.

Although he was facing the back of the boat, Tom could tell by the shoreline spreading out behind it that he was nearing the mouth of the river. The current created by the river emptying into the bay was pushing back at him, and it was getting harder to make any headway against the tide.

In the past half hour, the sun had burned the mist off the water, and now, as he peered ahead over his shoulder, he could see up the river to where the water curved around the next bend. The current had slowed some since the last time he had been here, but it was still too strong to row the boat any further than that bend.

Pulling hard on the paddles, he angled towards the riverbank, heading for a small stretch of sandy shoreline where he had left his boat in the past. When he felt the bottom rake the soft sand, he jumped into the shallow water and hauled it up onto the beach. Lifting out the rope that was tied to the stem, he secured the other end to a tree.

Tom knocked out the wooden plug at the back of the boat, and drained out the water that had leaked in through the seams. "I've got to do some work on that when I get back," he muttered.

Hauling his back pack from the front of the boat and dropping it on the sand, he reached under the seat and lifted out the flintlock. Settling the pack comfortably on his back, he balanced the long gun in his right hand, and trudged into the woods. He hiked along the path worn down over the years by settlers and Indians alike as they followed the river upstream.

The sun had finally cleared the horizon, sending golden rays sparkling and dancing off the surface of the swiftly moving river. Thick leafy branches of birch and aspen overhung the path around him so the river was often hidden from view. The early morning sun was already warming up the day, forcing Tom to unbutton the front of his wool jacket, as he walked. With his mind occupied with the work he had to do today he absentmindedly scratched at his long shaggy beard as he walked.

As he broke around the final bend in the trail, he could see salmon jumping through the layers of his weir out on the river. That's a good sign, he thought excitedly, there should be lots of fish in the weir, and it was just a matter of dipping out the first load. This was going to be easy! With the anticipation of a quick catch, he quickened his step, he didn't want any of them to escape.

Close to the river bank, he propped the gun against a large fir tree and shrugged off his back pack, letting it fall to the ground. He peeled off his coat, tossed it aside, and reached up to retrieve his dip net from where it hung in the tree. Something registered as not being right, but he shrugged it off, and hurried towards the river where he could see the weir was teaming with salmon, dozens of them, struggling to swim upstream. He smiled eagerly.

He was about to step from the bank onto the side of the wooden weir when the pieces clicked together in his mind. Someone had built a blind near where the path entered the clearing. Slowly he turned, sensing he was no longer alone. There, at the edge of the trees, just thirty feet away, was a young Indian girl.

He found himself staring down the shaft of an arrow, just inches below her dark angry eyes. In that instant before the release, he clearly saw the fine lines of tension in her red ochre painted face, and the taunt muscles of her bare straining arms, as she pulled the bow string tight. Three Indian men stood at her side, with their bows at the ready. Faint smiles creased their red leathery faces.

Tom's throat suddenly went dry. Even though he wanted to, he couldn't swallow. A cold bead of sweat trickled slowly down his back underneath his shirt. His eyes flickered to the tree where his flintlock stood, some 20 paces away. His ears picked up the sharp twang of the release of the bow string as the arrow bit deep into his chest. Staggering back he stumbled and fell to one knee, letting the dip net slip through his fingers onto the ground. Time slowed. Looking down, he curiously touched the long wooden shaft sticking out of his chest. His mind registered the details of the black and white goose feathers lashed to the end of the shaft. Blood dripped from his hand where it touched the front of his shirt, but he didn't feel any pain.

His mind was a jumble of confusion. He knew there was something he needed to do. It was there, just out of reach. The gun! I've got to get the gun!

Clumsily pushing to his feet, he tried to run for the gun, but on the first step, he felt the impact of another arrow, and found himself on both knees this time. He knew he wasn't going to make it. Using what little strength he had left, he wearily lifted his head, and watched over his shoulder as she purposely walked toward him with a long handled knife in her hand. He noticed the blade was spotted with rust and what appeared to be dried blood. He hoped she wasn't going to use that dirty knife on him.

He had heard that their custom was to take their victims heads as trophies, and the acid taste of fear welled up in his throat, making him gag. Unable to keep his head up, he let it drop until he was staring at her dirty, red, caribou skin moccasins.

Vaguely he heard them talking in their strange tongue, as the rabbit foot charm was roughly yanked from his neck. The girl grabbed a handful of his long scraggily beard, and pulled his head up until he was gazing directly into her hate filled black eyes. That momentary connection crossed the language barrier, and he knew with a certainty that she was the one from last winter. The one that he'd thought hadn't got away. With horror he felt the touch of the cold blade on his exposed throat as he slid into inescapable darkness.

Chapter 6
1789
Buggishaman

Two weeks had passed since she killed the Buggishaman. She remembered the fear she had seen in his eyes when she pulled his head back. The image had stayed with her. Sometimes it filled her dreams. It had not given her the satisfaction she had expected it would, but it was something that had to be done to give her father peace. She had received confirmation when she heard the moisamadrook howl as her uncle raised the Buggishaman's head on a long pole at the edge of camp. That had made it right.

That night Beeroute had told everyone the story at the campfire. He told how they had built the hiding place near the Buggishaman's fishing spot and how they waited three days for him to appear. He told how Shanadee had avenged her father and everyone clapped and told her what an honorable thing she had done. Everyone had seemed very happy for her. It had made her feel very proud.

Today she was hunting alone just as she had done every day since the killing. Her knees were cushioned by the soft covering of moss that surrounded the base of the short spruce bush. Its thick branches extended all the way to the ground providing her with a good hiding place from her prey. Sitting back on her heels, she loosely gripped her hathemay in the palm of her left hand. A blunt-headed arrow that she used for small game was already notched onto the string, ready to be drawn, and sent flying at the unsuspecting prey. A second arrow lay on the ground next to her knees, within easy reach. She had been kneeling here motionless for so long, the song birds she had originally disturbed had returned to the trees around her. They were unknowingly providing additional cover for her. Their constant fluttering and chattering signaled to the creatures on the ground that there was no danger lurking nearby.

She had become one with her surroundings. The cheerful sounds of the summer birds, and the fragrant smells of new growth that filled the air around her, made her feel happy, something she hadn't felt much of in a while. This was the part of the hunt she loved best. She had learned to make herself a part of the forest at her father's side. He had taught her the ways of the hunt, from the time she was strong enough to draw a hathemay. He had taken her hunting with him since she was old enough to walk. Since then she had watched and mimicked everything he did.

"You only need to be patient, little one," he said. He'd always called her "little one." It was his pet name for her.

She remembered not liking it at first, but over the years she had grown to love it when he called her that. It was their special bond. Something special between the two of them. She wished he were here with her now. Thinking of him drained away some of the happiness she had been feeling, but she had some great memories of their time together. She found herself trying to spend more time thinking of the good times these days. After all she had avenged his death, and that was the most she could do for him.

Her wandering mind returned to the hunt. Her trained eye could see the signs indicating the rabbit run was getting lots of use. Moving her eyes along the path, she could see the recently chewed young tree shoots. The exposed ends were still white, like broken bones protruding through torn skin, not yet dried enough to darken the color. It's only a matter of time and they will come to me, she thought, as she soundlessly blew away a loose strand of hair drifting annoyingly across her eyes.

She was about to give in and tuck the hair back into her braid, when a small movement at the extreme edge of her vision caught her attention, At first it was just a brief glimpse of shadow, there for a second and then gone again. Then two large gray rabbits appeared, coming down the run on her left. They were moving in short hops, stopping to nibble on fresh shoots as they came. They were unhurried and showed no sign that they had any sense of danger.

Shanadee watched in absolute stillness from behind the low spruce bush. They were close enough for her to see the pink inside the leading rabbit's ears, as they swiveled front and back, constantly searching the air, listening for any sound of danger. Each strand of its long twitching whiskers became clearly visible, as she focused totally on her prey.

She picked the trailing rabbit as her first target. It would give her a better chance to get both of them. Slowly she pulled the hathemay string taunt, held it there for a second, and then launched the arrow with a soft twang. The second arrow that had been lying on the ground was notched and airborne almost before the first found its mark. The two rabbits toppled over in quick succession.

Shanadee pushed to her feet and stepped out of her hiding place, stretching the stiffness out of her cramped legs as she walked. Using the small club that was hanging at her side, she quickly dealt each rabbit a final death blow to the head. Kill your game cleanly her father had taught her. Do not make the animals suffer, and do not kill more than you need, he would tell her. They are provided for your food, but you must respect their lives also, she could almost hear him say.

Retrieving the two arrows, she checked them for damage. Finding none, she slipped them back into her leather quiver. She picked up the rabbits by their back legs, tied their feet together with a thin string of root, and hung them from her belt. Tucking the stray hair back into her braid, she settled the hathemay comfortably over her shoulder, turned, and headed back towards camp under a cloudless blue sky. It had been another good hunt, she thought happily. Father would have enjoyed it.

Providing food for her family was now resting squarely on her shoulders. Since Father had been killed she had become the main provider for her mother and brothers. Her brother Timmwall was young, and still learning. There were only four grown men in the band at their camp, and they had to find food for their own families. That didn't include Old Pandelle, of course, but he was crippled and couldn't hunt. Uncle Beeroute tried to help when he could, but most of the responsibility fell on Shanadee. At least it was something she enjoyed doing, and she was good at it too. She always brought something back to camp.

There weren't enough of them in the band to herd the caribou as in the old days, so they had to rely on hunting individual animals, and that made it a whole lot harder to get meat. Rabbits and other small animals would supplement their diet for now. She knew she could find plenty of them.

In a couple of weeks the band would move further inland and meet up with other bands for the annual caribou hunt. Shanadee was looking forward to the hunt. She would get to be in it this year. This would be the first time for her. She felt excited as she thought of it and smiled as she walked along the trail.

She had heard the tales of the great hunts of the past, while sitting around the evening campfires. Old Pandelle loved to tell of times when the caribou ran in huge herds. Way too many to count, he'd say, spreading his arms wide. He'd describe all the work they had to do to build the natural fences by knocking down trees along the river banks. These fences ran for miles, and were used to herd the caribou into corrals where they could be easily taken. It took many people to keep these fences repaired, he'd say. There just weren't enough people anymore, so the hunts were much smaller. That was a time when our people covered the land, and we had it all to ourselves. That was back when your grandparents were young, he would say to her.

Pandelle was the storyteller of the band. He had lost the use of his left leg a couple of years earlier. No one knew what had happened or what had caused it. It had started out with a limp but it had quickly worsened until he had no control over it, and finally he had to use sticks to keep from falling. Despite this, he kept the smaller children entertained with his colorful story telling. It was a common sight to see him hobbling around camp with the smaller children in tow. They began calling him "old Pandelle", and the name stuck.

Now that he could no longer join in the hunt, Pandelle spent much of his time hammering out arrowheads from metal they had taken from the Buggishaman. He supplied Shanadee with all her arrow tips, in fact he had been working on some for her when she left camp this morning. He was using pieces of animal traps they had found on one of the trips to the coast last spring.

Shanadee had gone upriver today to hunt. None of the band had ventured down river for a couple of weeks, not since she had killed the Buggishaman and avenged her father's killing. They wanted to avoid the Buggishaman as much as they could. It was not safe to go downriver or anywhere near the coast right now. Shanadee touched the dark brown rabbit foot hanging from the string around her neck. It was her connection to her father; the only thing she had left from him. She remembered the feeling of delight when she had ripped it from the settler's neck. She had been so happy to get it back. Feeling the soft fur between her fingers took her back to those happy days with her father, before the Buggishaman had messed everything up.

The cloudless sky allowed the heat of the sun to soak through her cloak as she walked and it was making her feel warm all over. It was a soothing feeling, almost making her drowsy as she strolled unhurriedly along the river path. It felt good after the bitterly cold days of winter. This was the best time of the year. She loved the long warm days of summer.

Stepping off the path, she sliced off a lump of dried sap that had seeped through the bark of a spruce tree and popped it in her mouth. At first it was brittle and broke into little pieces, but as she continued chewing it became gummy and solid. It was a good taste and would last most of the day.

Soon she would start taking Timmwall on her hunting trips with her. She would teach him as her father had taught her. There was much for him to learn. He was already doing well with his hathemay. The problem was he didn't like killing anything. It always upset him and he just didn't seem to have the stomach for it. He'd much rather work around the camp than hunt. He probably should have been a girl. She had no idea where his feelings came from, but she would have to do her best to change them. Timmwall would never survive if he couldn't hunt, and besides the band needed all the hunters they could get if they were going to get enough meat stored for the winter.

Shanadee was getting near home when she was suddenly startled from her thoughts by the pounding of the drum. It was the signal to run; the signal that there was trouble at the camp. A sense of dread tightened her chest and clutched her lower stomach. She broke into a run. Her mind was painting the worse possible picture. Her family was back there. Anything could have happened. The Buggishaman must be there. Please, no! Not that!

She only carried her short hunting hathemay. Her long hathemay and iron tipped arrows were back at camp. She was practically unarmed. Her only other weapon was a knife, but she raced along the path toward camp anyway.

Then she heard the dreaded popping of the gunshots, and the distant shouting in that strange language. The sounds gave her a new sense of urgency as her feet flew over the uneven ground. She had to get back there and help her family. She had to get them out of there. The noises scared her. They scared her, but they also made her angry. The Buggishaman was there at the camp. Recklessly she ran on towards the ominous sounds.

Racing around a sharp bend in the river path, she ran headlong into the first members of the band. They were strung out along the trail, desperately running away from the terror that had descended on the camp. Shanadee grabbed the arm of one of the running women and pulled her to a stop.

"Let me go! Let go of me," the woman screamed frantically.

"What happened?" Shanadee yelled into her panic stricken face as the woman tried to yank her arm free.

"The Buggishaman were in the camp before we knew they were around. There was no warning! There's a bunch of them. They have guns! They are shooting everyone," she screamed hysterically, still struggling to pull her arm free, as others rushed by.

"Where is Mother? Where are Timmwall and Jaywritt?" Shanadee shouted into the frightened woman's face.

"Back there. They got them before they had a chance to run. Manddilleeitt sounded the drum. She saved us." The woman jumped as more shots rang out from the direction of the camp. "There is your little brother," she pointed with her free arm back down the path at the little boy. "You must take him and run," she said urgently, as she finally yanked her arm free of Shanadee's grip. With wild uncontrolled terror in her eyes, she turned, bolted up the river path, and disappeared around the bend.

Shanadee ran down the path to her little brother and protectively gripped his hand. She pulled him to the side of the path, and watched as more of the terror stricken tribe members ran by them in total abandonment. She did not see Uncle Beeroute among the fleeing band. Maybe he was helping mother. Mother would have trouble running with her bad back. Looking down river, she could see dark heavy smoke rising above the trees where their camp was. That didn't look good. She was scared for her mother and her brother. She could only hope they had made it into the woods somehow. Looking down at the weeping child so fiercely squeezing her hand, she wished she could go on down to the camp and kill some of those white devils, but it was not to be.

She had to protect her little brother now. That was the only choice she had. She desperately hoped the woman was wrong, and that the others had escaped into the safety of the woods. With resignation she turned and led him up the path in the direction the others had fled. She would come back to the camp later in the evening, just before it got dark.

Because Jaywritt could not walk as fast as her Shanadee carried him over some of the rougher parts of the trail. They were on the trail alone and she didn't want to take the chance the Buggishaman might be following them. She found where the others had left the trail and followed them into the deep woods. By the time they reached the clearing where the others had gathered, Shanadee was exhausted. Worriedly looking around at the little group she saw everyone was there except her mother Manddilleeitt, her brother Timmwall, her uncle Beeroute, the wife of Jeddilledt and old Pandelle. They should have been there by now. The woman on the trail had told her the Buggishaman had killed some of the band. It must be them. Where else could they be?

"You brought this on us," screamed one of the women, shaking her finger at Shanadee from across the clearing. "Why did you have to kill that Buggishaman? Did it bring your father back to you? What did you gain from it? Now look what has happened. This is all, your fault."

Gently slipping his arm around her shoulder, her husband, Addrondett, said softly, "it is our way Ofeius. The Buggishaman killed Nanolute. Shanadee just avenged his death. It needed to be done so Nanolute's spirit could rest. Come away now and leave her alone."

Shanadee stood there at the edge of the clearing, in stunned silence. She knew in her heart the woman was probably right. This *was* her fault and there was no way to fix it. She had brought this down on their heads and made things so much worse for the band. More lives were probably lost because of what she had done. Five of the band members were still missing. Three of them were members of her family. What have I done?

"Why did she say those mean things to you, Shanadee?" a small voice said from behind her.

Turning around Shanadee forced a smile to her face and said, "She didn't mean it Jaywritt. She's upset that the Buggishaman drove us from our camp. That's all."

"But why is she blaming you. You weren't even there! That's not fair."

"I know. She's just really scared little brother. We all are."

"Stupid old woman!" he muttered, glaring across the clearing. 'Where are mother and Timmwall? Why aren't they here yet?"

"They had to run into the woods to escape. They will be here soon."

"I hope they are alright."

"I hope so too."

Shanadee looked across at the small cooking fire the others were sitting around. I guess we are far enough away that the Buggishaman won't see the smoke here she thought. She noticed they were burning dry sticks to reduce the smoke so there was very little to see anyway.

"Let's get some wood and start our own fire," she said.

Taking Jaywritt by the hand, she led him back into the woods at the edge of the clearing, and they began gathering dry sticks and peeling strips of birch rind from the trees.

Shanadee set up away from the rest of the group. She didn't want anything to do with any of them right now. Ofeius wouldn't be the only one who blamed her. They probably all did for all she knew. It was better that she stay away from them for now.

She did pull a burning stick from the other fire and used it to light the birch rind and soon had their fire blazing.

Then she set about preparing the rabbits. First she made a cut around each of the back legs of the first rabbit, just above the paw joint. Then she began peeling the skin down the legs.

"OK. Hold on to it Jaywritt."

Jaywritt gripped a furry paw in each hand and Shanadee tugged the skin down the body and over the head. Laying the skinned rabbit aside she quickly repeated the procedure on the second rabbit. She turned the furs right side out and put them aside for drying. Next she removed the insides, separating the guts from the heart and liver. Those she put aside to cook later. They were delicacies to be savored. Then she mounted the rabbits on long sticks and bent them over the open fire to roast them. All of this, she did mechanically, forcing herself not to think of her mother and brother. There was no point getting Jaywritt upset, not until she knew for sure, although she feared the worst.

When the rabbits finished roasting, Shanadee cut up the first one and shared it with Jaywritt. Before they began to eat she held out the second rabbit to Jaywritt and said, "Take this one to Ofeius and her family."

"But she said mean things to you Shanadee."

"I told you she didn't mean it Jaywritt. We have enough for us. It is only right to share what we have."

"But, why give it to *her*?"

"Because we are a small band and we have to be friends and work together."

"Oh, alright, if you say so," he said grudgingly.

"I do say so. Hurry now before your rabbit gets cold."

She watched him as he walked across the clearing to where Ofeius, Addrondett and her son Crandulait and daughter Serondius sat around their cooking fire. It's alright for Ofeius, she thought. She still has all her family with her. What have I got? Just my little brother and me, that's all I have left. I won't be mad at her but that doesn't mean I have to like her.

She watched as Jaywritt handed the rabbit to Ofeius. Ofeius did not look her way as she held out her hand and accepted the gift, but her husband nodded in her direction and smiled in acknowledgement. The rabbit wasn't much but it helped. Although Ofeius words hurt her, she knew it was important not to let it come between them. They would need every member of the band if they were going to get through the next winter. Fighting Ofeius would only make things worse for all of them.

Pulling her eyes away from the group, she looked at the woods surrounding the clearing, hoping to see the other band members appear. Still there was no sign of anyone. She desperately needed to see her family walk out of the woods, yet in her heart she knew it wasn't going to happen. She wiped a stray tear from her cheek as Jaywritt returned to the fire, picked up some of the roasted rabbit and popped it in his mouth.

As she chewed on the warm rabbit meat her mind drifted to Uncle Beeroute. He had been one of the strongest hunters in the band and, unless he showed up soon, she knew, because of her hunting skills, she, along with the other three men, would now be the main providers for the small band. Looking around the clearing she counted fourteen including herself and Jaywritt. Not a very big group she thought. It's not going to be easy to get the food we need to get through next winter. We've probably already lost what we had stored at the camp.

Weighed down by the dark cloud of sadness that seemed to be pressing in from all sides, Shanadee went through the motions of helping Jaywritt finish up his meal. She did not want him to know what had happened until she was sure. He was too young.

"Jaywritt, I am going to go look for mother and Timmwall," she said as they were finishing the last of the rabbit.

"Can I come?"

"No little brother. It may not be safe yet. The Buggishaman might still be there."

"But I'm not scared, Shanadee," he said bravely, as he wiped rabbit grease from his chin with his chubby fist.

"I know, Jaywritt", she smiled at him, "but I need to go alone. I want you to stay here with the other families. It's safe for you here. Besides it will be a lot faster if I go by myself."

"What if you don't come back? What do I do then?

"What do you mean? Why wouldn't I come back?

"The Buggishaman might get you too."

Shanadee stared at her brother. Maybe he understands more than I think he does. Maybe there is no need to shelter him. Aloud she said to him. "I will be careful, and I will come back. I promise."

"You promise sister?"

"I promise."

"OK then," he said as he ran over to join the other families at their fire.

Shanadee borrowed a long hathemay and some iron tipped arrows from one of the men, and strode quickly across the clearing into the woods. The band members were already busy cutting poles to build new mamateeks to replace those abandoned in their hasty retreat from the Buggishaman. Life had to go on. It was the way it had to be.

Shanadee avoided the river path and made her way through the deeper woods. She made a wide circuit, and approached the camp from the opposite side from where the Buggishaman would have entered. Standing motionless behind a thick spruce tree, she listened quietly as smoke from the smoldering fires at the campsite drifted around her. The swirling smoke carried smells that were not familiar to her. A peculiar scent that reminded her of cooked meat, but not the kind she had ever smelled before.

All was quiet. The only sound that came from the camp was the angry screeching of crows. It seemed that the Buggishaman had left.

Quietly she notched an arrow in the hathemay, and cautiously entered the campsite near her father's burial hut. It, like everything else, had been burnt to the ground. Shanadee avoided looking at the mound of ash and smoldering wood in the middle. Her eyes swept around the campsite and she remained absolutely still. The muscles of her arms and legs were tensed like a tight hathemay string. Hearing only the sounds of small animals and birds, she knew she was alone and she allowed the tension to drain from her body as she stood there.

The tall ceremonial pole that had been stuck in the ground near the burial hut was lying nearby. She had skinned all the bark from it with her knife, before Beeroute had placed the severed head of the fisherman at the top. This was done to make her father's journey to the land of Gossett easier. The head was no longer there.

She found Old Pandelle in the first burned out mamateek. He lay face down, his twisted legs covered with burning poles from the collapsed mamateek. It looked as though he had fallen across the threshold. His long white hair was stained red. Shanadee knelt next to him and lifted the hair from his face. There was no face there! He had been smashed and beaten beyond recognition. Shocked, Shanadee let the hair fall from her hand. She saw the steel trap on the ground next to him. It was covered in blood and bits of white hair. In horror she backed away. Now she knew what she had smelled. She spat on the ground trying to rid herself of the disgusting taste in her mouth.

She turned and looked across the clearing. Her family's mamateek was just a smoldering heap of ash as well. Manddilleeitt and the other woman were lying near the smoking ruins. Manddilleeitt still clutched the little drum in her left hand. Her vacant unmoving eyes stared up at her daughter. Blood had caked around the gaping hole in her throat where the bullet had exited. Shanadee dropped to her knees. What she had feared the most had come to pass. She tenderly cradled her mother's face in her hands, and the tears she had suppressed all day suddenly arrived in a cresting wave that crashed over her. She was no longer aware of anything around her. She was overwhelmed with the need to feel her mother's arms around her. Falling on the ground in anguish, she stretched out next to Manddilleeitt, wrapped her arms around her, rested her head on her mother's lifeless chest and cried. She cried until there were no more tears left, until only dry sobs wracked her body.

"Why, Mother, why?" she sobbed. "Why did you leave me now?"

Finally she pushed herself to a kneeling position. She felt exhausted and empty. She did not want to leave her mother but she had to find the others. With her knife she cut a piece of cloth from the bottom of her cloak and covered Manddilleeitt's face.

Standing to her feet she looked around the smoky campsite. She spotted Timmwall closer to the woods. Her brother had been shot in the back. He lay with his hathemay still clutched tightly in his hand. She wondered if he had used it; if he had overcome his aversion to killing at the end. She hoped so.

Her uncle, Beeroute, lay on the riverbank, partially in the water. The river current tugged at him, moving his legs as if there was still life there. He had been shot as well. There were no weapons around him. He had probably been surprised at the river with no chance to defend the family.

Shanadee looked around for something against which to vent her anger. There was nothing. The Buggishaman had all gone, destroying her family on their way. Nothing would ever be the same again. In frustration she threw back her head and released a primal scream into the sky, frightening the scavenging crows from their perch high in the trees behind her. In one fluid motion she whirled and shot, silencing one of the scolding black birds with an arrow through its chest. She watched it flutter and plummet to the ground.

The Buggishaman had raided the camp before they left. They had burned all the mamateeks, and taken most of their supply of meat, as well as the drying caribou skins. Her eyes took all this in as she surveyed the little camp from where she stood. It had all been destroyed. Those who had survived the slaughter were now in real danger of not having enough supplies to get through the winter. Even in the midst of her overwhelming grief Shanadee could see the dangerous position they were in and the urgent need to find new food supplies.

Shanadee walked into the woods and recovered a hathemay and stash of arrows she had hidden in the branches of a tree just outside the clearing. It felt more comfortable in her hand than the borrowed one. Returning to the clearing, the bitter taste of anger once again welled up in her throat and she spat forcefully on the ground. She hated the Buggishaman. Even more she hated the fact that she could do nothing about it without bringing more death and destruction on her tribe.

In her anger she thought of following them. She would be able to catch them and to kill some of them, she knew. They wouldn't expect anyone to follow. That would be the last thing they would be thinking about after seeing the terrified tribe bolt into the woods. Ofeius' words rang in her ears, and she knew she couldn't do this. As much as she wanted to hunt them and kill them all, she couldn't risk it. She had to consider the rest of the tribe, especially her little brother. He was all she had left. It was up to her to protect him.

The only option left to her was to totally avoid the Buggishaman. This was not getting any easier. The Buggishaman was venturing further inland all the time in his persistent search for more furs. Contact with him was inevitable.

Standing in the midst of the destruction, Shanadee was overcome with a dark, overbearing sense of loss that left a gnawing emptiness deep inside of her. This had been a slaughter, a mindless killing for no good end. Why would they do this thing? She went to Timmwall, lifted him as much as she could and dragged his limp body to where their mother lay on the ground.

Shanadee sat on the burned ground next to them. She wept again as she rocked gently back and forth in the smoking ruins. Her family had been wiped out and she had not been there to help when they needed her the most.

"I could have made a difference," she sobbed aloud, although her hollow words gave her little comfort now. "I could have saved you."

Forcing her body to move, she pushed herself to her feet. She lifted the cloth from her mother's face and went to the river to soak it. With the wet cloth she gently washed the blood and soot from her mother's face. "I will come back for you," she said through her tears.

Behind her she heard the snap of a twig and she whirled around, slipping the hathemay from her shoulder as she turned. Crouching there with an arrow in her hand, she found herself face to face with the gray moisamadrook. He was no more than five strides away. She could see the yellow teeth through the slight curl of his upper lip. A low rumble came from deep in its wide chest. She knew her father's spirit had taken up residence there, but it was still a wild animal and maybe his spirit wasn't strong enough to control its savage nature.

Slowly she raised the hathemay and the moisamadrook sat back on its haunches, taking a much less threatening position. It seemed to be telling her it had nothing but friendly intentions. Looking into his unblinking eyes she said, "I see you father. Take care of mother and Timmwall."

She stood to her feet and lowered the hathemay. Turning her back on the moisamadrook, she moved around the clearing and gathered up what she could find. The metal pans she set aside to pick up later, but the arrow and spear heads she dropped in her shoulder bag.

The sun was setting when she set out for the new camp. She turned and looked back one last time before leaving the clearing. The moisamadrook was still sitting there, quietly watching her.

Tomorrow she would return with the band, and bury her family.

Chapter 7
1791
Move to the Interior

During the two years since the fateful raid on their camp by the eight Buggishaman, the little band had not fared so well. That first winter had been one of the worst Shanadee could remember. The loss of their winter's store of meat to the raiders had brought them near to starvation. There had not been enough time to replace the supply before the winter freeze up, and the group was forced to ration what little they could find. Shanadee had spent much of her time away from camp, attempting to find small game to get them through. Most of her days were spent hunting and roaming the woods close to the camp. She had honed her skills with her hathemay until she could hit moving targets as well as she could hit motionless ones. Sometimes she would let birds take flight before shooting them, just to test herself. She knew her father would have been proud of her.

They were lucky that they all made it through that winter, but they did; a whole lot thinner but alive. That was what really mattered, the fact that they hadn't lost anyone, thought Shanadee.

They built a new camp that summer, back on the banks of the river but further upstream from the camp which the Buggishaman had raided.

It had been a good summer for the band and they had been much better prepared going into last winter. Hunting had been good and they had been able to store plenty of meat meaning food was no longer a problem. Their problem, when it arrived, came from a completely different direction.

It all had started with the persistent coughing. That had been the first sign of the dreaded disease of the Buggishaman. Shanadee remembered lying in her wigwam at night being unable to sleep because of the nonstop coughing coming from a wigwam built next to theirs. Burying her head in the furs hadn't helped much either. She just hadn't been able to drown out that sleep killing sound.

Beeroute's wife, Ebanatho, had agreed to move the couple's two children in with her and her two boys to make sure they weren't exposed to the coughing disease consuming their parents. The band had then turned the couple's wigwam into a sweat lodge. Round river stones were dug up from the snow covered riverbank and placed in a trench around the fire. Water was then poured on the heated stones, filling the wigwam with swirling clouds of hot steam. This was to help drive out the sickness that had entered their bodies.

Ofeius had taken charge and kept the steam going for days. She also prepared food for the couple and tried to make them as comfortable as she could. No one else had been allowed to enter their wigwam. She had administered liquid concoctions for days, but the disease advanced relentlessly until both of them were too weak to swallow anything.

They both lost their battle on the same day.

Shanadee had helped collect everything that the ill-fated couple had touched. It had all been placed in the wigwam next to their bodies, and the wigwam had been ignited and burned to the ground. She remembered standing holding Jaywritt's hand and having to back away from the heat as the fire swept up the birch bark walls and consumed the wigwam in minutes.

Finally the days had begun to grow warmer, the snow started to slowly melt away, and the snapping and groaning of the shifting ice on the river announced that spring was moving in. Those days had brought hope for the band; a realization that the long, crippling winter was almost behind them and the chance to rebuild lay ahead.

Spring, however, was not to be without its share of tragedy either.

She remembered the morning Crandulait had crossed the frozen river in search of small game. It was a good area to hunt. Shanadee had hunted there herself many times since they had set up camp at the river. In fact, she and

Crandulait had taken down a caribou there a few weeks before.

It was quiet and peaceful country, undisturbed by the Buggishaman who had never ventured this far up river.

Later that evening, Addrondett and Jeddilledt had been standing down at the riverbank when Crandulait emerged from the woods on the other side of the frozen river. Seeing them, he had waved and held up several small animals he was carrying on a stick over his shoulder. It seemed he'd had a successful day of hunting. They said he had shouted something but he was too far away for them to understand what he had said.

Crandulait had stepped onto the ice and started across. He had reached about halfway, when suddenly the air was split with a sharp crack that sounded like the Buggishaman's gun.

Shanadee had been inside her wigwam with Jaywritt. She remembered how scared she had been when she heard the sound. Her first thought was that the Buggishaman was here. She remembered shouting at Jaywritt to stay inside as she raced out the door with her hathemay in her hand. Her relief at finding no Buggishaman had been quickly swept away as she looked out across the frozen river to see what everyone was staring at. Out in the middle of the river the ice shifted with another loud crack and opened up beneath Crandulait's feet. In a moment he had been swallowed up by the swirling water and disappeared from the sight of the stunned watchers at the campsite.

Shanadee had known Crandulait from birth; in fact, they had been born the same summer. Ofeius and Addrondett had searched for their son for days but after the river took him underneath the ice he was never found.

With three more of the band gone, there were only eleven remaining. That left her, Addrondett and Jeddilledt to hunt for the band. The two older boys were learning, but they wouldn't be much help for the winter ahead. It was shaping up to be another hard winter.

Shanadee was mulling all of these things over in her head as she stirred a pot of meat stew over the open fire at the center of the wigwam. She hardly noticed the mouthwatering savory smell that filled the room. Jaywritt sat on the bed of green boughs watching her. The hathemay she had made for him lay on the ground near his side. He never ventured far without it.

Noticing Shanadee was looking at him, he grabbed the hathemay, leapt to his feet and began to dance around her, pretending to shoot invisible game. Shanadee laughed at his antics as he leaped and ran around the wigwam until he could run no more. He collapsed and rolled on the ground in exhaustion.

"You will be a mighty hunter someday," she teased him. "You will hunt the caribou and the great white bear. People will say, come see, this is Jaywritt the mighty."

Jaywritt got up and came to stand at Shanadee's side. He was no taller than she was in her kneeling position.

Wrapping his arms around her neck, he gave her a fierce hug. "I want to be just like you, sister," he said.

Shanadee smiled at him and kissed his forehead. She wondered to herself what would become of them. She wondered if they would survive long enough for her to see him grow.

Later that same evening, the other members of the band joined Shanadee in her wigwam. Just as they did on so many evenings before, they sat around the fire and talked of the good times; times long ago, before the Buggishaman had found their place. They talked of happier times when their people covered the land and were too many to count. They repeated the stories they had been told by their parents and grandparents and in more recent times by Old Pandelle. Now that he was gone Jeddilledt had taken on the storyteller's role. This was how they had kept their history alive down through time, passing it to their children through their stories.

Tonight, however, it didn't take long for the talking to turn to their plight, and how they would fare during the coming winter.

Shanadee sat quietly, listening to the conversation going on around her in the crowded wigwam.

'Does anyone think there's even a chance we will to be able to gather enough food for the winter?" asked Ebanatho.

"Well we are certainly way behind right now." responded Addrondett. "After all, there are only three of us left to hunt, and that makes it a whole lot harder to get the bigger animals like the caribou."

"We have to get at least five or six caribou. If we don't we will never have enough meat to get us through," Jeddilledt added.

"The other problem is that we can't go to the coast to hunt the monau because of the Buggishaman," Addrondett continued."

"No that would be much too dangerous," said Ebanatho, "it's not worth the risk."

"Well then, what are we going to do?" asked Ofeius worriedly. "We have to have food, and we have no idea how long the winter will last."

"We will just have to do the best we can," replied Jeddilledt.

Finally Shanadee broke her silence. "We must make the trip to the Great Lake," she said.

The other four adults looked at her thoughtfully. She was not yet an adult but she had earned her place as a hunter and provider for the group and, even though she was young, they recognized her as one of them. There was no acknowledged chief of the band and they shared the leadership roles equally.

Normally Shanadee had no interest in being a part of the leadership of the group. She was more than content to look after her little brother and let the others make the decisions for the band. That was unless they were missing the obvious, like now.

As she had been quietly listening to the conversation, she had been looking around at the ten faces around her fire, and it was with a sinking heart that she had realized there would not be many more winters for them if they didn't join with a bigger group. They were mostly women and children. They needed the help and safety of a larger group if they were going to have any chance at all of surviving.

In the past few weeks other Beothuk had passed through their camp on the way upriver to the Great Lake. Shanadee had listened to their tales of being hunted and shot at by the Buggishaman. Avoiding contact altogether was becoming the only safe thing to do. Of course, this also meant there was no safe access to the food supply at the coast and that was making their situation much worse.

"That's way too far. It would take us a couple of weeks at least," said Ofeius. "No. That's not a good idea."

Shanadee had expected some opposition from Ofeius. She worried about everything. It was as though she thought it was her job to worry. Besides, it was her nature to oppose anything Shanadee said anyway. She still blamed her for causing their problems, and she wasn't about to let someone as young as Shanadee tell her what to do.

"Perhaps it is a good idea." Jeddilledt said thoughtfully. "With a larger group we could do a proper caribou hunt."

"And we wouldn't have to live in fear of the Buggishaman every day," Ebanatho said. "That would be a good thing."

"It would be good not to have to be looking over your shoulder all the time."

"How do we know the tribe is at the Great Lake anyway? What if we go all that way and find no one there? We'd be better off using the time to gather more food. I still think it is a bad idea, and a big waste of time too," Ofeius responded.

"There is always some of the tribe at the Great Lake, Ofeius," said Addrondett. "It has always been that way. Besides, we know the groups that passed through here will be there."

"It is all we can do," said Ebanatho. "I don't think we will all make it through the winter if we stay here."

Shanadee stayed out of the conversation. She thought it would be best to let the others come to the same conclusion by themselves.

"It is no longer safe here, anyway. I worry about the children," Ebanatho continued.

"Why isn't it safe here? We haven't seen a Buggishaman in almost two years," Ofeius countered.

"We know they are moving upriver all the time. It's only a matter of time before they get here."

"We need to protect the children," said Jeddilledt. "Shanadee is right. We must go to the Lake."

"Yes. She is right. We must go," agreed Addrondett.

Ebanatho nodded in agreement as well.

Ofeius shrugged reluctantly. "I guess the decision is made. I still don't like it."

"Then it is decided," said Shanadee. "We should go soon."

They talked late into the night, working out a plan for the trip inland. They decided it would be best to make the journey in a series of short trips, relaying the supplies from camp to camp with rest times in between. This way it would take a couple of weeks to get there, but it would make it easier for the children. During the rest times they would hunt fresh meat for the camp.

The plan was to load the larger pieces of meat into tapaithooks and pull them up the river as far as the falls. Everyone would carry a full load on their backs, and return the following day for another. This would be repeated, until everything they needed was moved.

The children had all fallen asleep by the time they had finished planning. The smaller ones had to be carried back to their wigwams in their parent's arms when they finally left Shanadee's wigwam late that night.

Shanadee spent the next few days packing up their things, and getting Jaywritt ready for the trek up river. His excitement was almost infectious. He thought it would be a great adventure and he bounced around the wigwam like one of those rubber balls taken from the settlers. He was too young to understand why they were leaving or how long and difficult the trip might be.

Before they settled down to sleep the last night, Shanadee applied a fresh coat of odemet to both herself and Jaywritt.

"Why do you paint us like this, sister?" he asked.

"This red color makes you special, Jaywritt."

"How does red make me special? Everybody is red! Blue would be special!"

"Not just you silly," laughed Shanadee. "I meant all of us. It sets us apart from the other Indians and the Buggishaman. It shows everyone you are a Beothuk."

"It makes us look different?"

"Yes it does. But what is more important is that it makes it easier for the Great Spirit to see us. That way, He can protect us from our enemies."

"Oh," he said thoughtfully as he stretched out on his bed and closed his eyes. "Night Shanadee," he said sleepily, "I like different."

Shanadee smiled as she poured the leftover powder into a leather pouch to take on the trip. It would probably be some time before they would get back to the coast to get more.

She was still smiling to herself in the dark as she drifted off to sleep. She was glad she had her little brother with her. He always seemed to make the days a little brighter.

Early the next morning two of the tapaithooks were loaded with their remaining meat supplies. Two of the older boys and two of the older girls were given the responsibility to get them safely up river. The girls stayed in the water with each tapaithook. Their job was to steady it while the boys walked up river with long ropes that were attached to the boats. Once the rope had been stretched out to its full length, the boys began to pull the loaded tapaithooks up the river to where they were. The girls walked in waist high water holding on to the sides to keep them straight. This process would be repeated many times in the coming days.

The rest of the band stood on the bank and watched them pull the heavily loaded tapaithooks out of sight around the first bend in the river. Then they picked up their bundles and set out on the path that wound through the woods along the river's edge. Each of them was carrying as much as they could manage. Even the small children were given something to carry.

Earlier in the week, Shanadee had fashioned a rack from two long poles with a number of short sticks laced across them. Over this she had stretched a large caribou skin and tied it tight. This morning she took everything from their wigwam and stacked it on the rack. She tied a short rope, made to loop around her neck and under her arms, to both poles as she had seen her father do. Gripping a pole in each hand, she found it was easy to pull the load. Jaywritt trotted along the path ahead of her, carrying his hathemay in his hand, and some supplies in a small sack he had slung over his shoulder.

The group travelled slowly to allow the tapaithooks to keep up. They were not in a hurry. Camp would be struck wherever they were when the sun had crossed the sky.

Looking around her as she walked, Shanadee was struck by the beauty of the country she loved. Late spring had carpeted the land with fresh growth that embraced the travelers in its sweet and familiar scents, heralding in a season of new life and new beginnings. The path wove its way through tall white birches, laden with fluttering leaves unfolding and stretching to catch the warmth of the early morning sun. Overhead, the canopy of intertwined branches was filled with a concert of chirping birds. Behind her Ebanatho was singing softly and ahead Jaywritt was chattering happily to the other small boy in the group.

The much travelled trail followed along the path of the wide river, sometimes close to its banks, sometimes further inland. At those points close to the river the group would stop and check the progress of the tapaithooks. When they encountered rapids, they would help pull the boats along the shoreline with two people in the water steadying each tapaithook.

By evening of that first day the group was exhausted. Once they had the tapaithooks pulled out of the water they collapsed around the campfire and slept where they lay.

In the morning, the four adults and two of the teenagers made the trek back to the old camp to retrieve the remainder of their supplies. Jaywritt and the other young boy were left with Ofeius' daughter, Serondius. Serondius was the obvious choice. She was the one who had taken care of Jaywritt when Shanadee had been away from camp on her many hunting trips. She loved being around the younger children and was now considered the band's babysitter. The other teenage boy was left to guard the loaded tapaithooks and protect the meat from marauding animals.

After the adults had left, Shanadee took her hathemay and headed into the woods in search of small game.

Without the younger children and the tapaithooks, the trip back to the old camp was much faster, and the group returned late that night under the watchful eye of the full moon.

In their absence Shanadee had bagged a variety of birds and small animals and she had the fresh meat cooking when they returned.

After two more days of travel they reached the first falls. At first they could only hear the rumble of the crashing water and see the light mist swirling over the trees in the distance. As they grew closer the noise got louder until they had to shout to be heard. When the group on the trail finally reached the beach at the base of the falls they stood there in wonder, some of them seeing the sight for the first time. High above them, Shanadee thought maybe at least as tall as two mamateeks, the water rushed over the edge and fell with a thunderous crash onto the huge boulders strewn around the base of the steep cliffs. A fine mist swirled and danced over the boulders creating a colorful rainbow.

"Look Shanadee," shouted Jaywritt excitedly. "Look at all the colors."

"I see them little brother," she said as she dropped her load on the path and followed him down the beach to the water's edge.

"Where do the colors come from?

"It's the sun shining on the water that does it."

Picking up handfuls of small stones, Jaywritt and his friend began tossing them at the falls trying to hit the elusive rainbow.

Jeddilledt and Addrondett were already carrying the first load up the steep path snaking up the hillside to the top of the falls. The others began unloading the tapaithooks and carrying the supplies to the top. It was backbreaking work getting everything up the steep slope of the rocky trail. Manhandling the two tapaithooks over the obstacles without damaging them was even more difficult, and when they finished at the end of the day there was no energy left to cook. They chewed on dried meat, and were lulled asleep by the sound of the water rushing over the edge of the cliff.

It was midmorning before the tired group began to stir. The sun had already finished part of its journey across the sky and soon would be high overhead. The women prepared a meal while the men reloaded the tapaithooks. Jaywritt and the other little boy played with their hathemays, hunting and shooting imaginary game as they ran around the camp. Shanadee watched affectionately as she turned the meat that popped and sizzled on the hot stones ringing the fire. They were doing the right thing making the trip to the Great Lake. She knew it was going to be a good thing. Life would be better there.

After eating they packed everything up again and prepared to leave. The men launched the first tapaithook back into the river just a little upstream from the falls. The first two teenagers then took over and relayed it over the first leg of the day's trip.

The second one was launched and Shanadee and the others watched as the boy handling the line walked the shoreline, paying out the long rope until he reached its end. Serondius stood in waist high water holding the back of the tapaithook to keep it straight against the pull of the river's strong current. Just as her partner began to pull the tapaithook forward, she slipped and lost her footing on the slimy rocks of the riverbed. As she fell she grabbed the side of the tapaithook to steady herself, and the sudden unexpected motion yanked the rope from the boy's hands. The tapaithook swung sideways in the current, and was swiftly pulled into the center of the river, picking up speed as it was drawn downstream toward the falls.

The rest of the band standing on the riverbank watched in horror as the tragedy unfolded right there in front of them, helpless to do anything to stop it.

Serondius was still desperately hanging onto the side of the heavily laden tapaithook when its downriver charge was abruptly halted, as it slammed to a stop between two large boulders sticking out of the water just before the river plunged over the cliff. The tapaithook was hanging at the very edge of the falls.

Ofeius ran along the riverbank yelling encouragement to her daughter. The others stood frozen where they were.

The force of the water crashing over the edge of the falls pinned Serondius against the side of the tapaithook. Both her arms were locked over the edge of the tapaithook and around a seat. The racing water had torn away her cloak and was slowly and inevitably dragging her underneath the boat. The muscles in her shoulders bulged with the strain as she frantically tried to hang on. Across the rushing water her eyes met her mothers in an agonizing plea for help.

The pressure of the hurtling water had been slowly bending the frail tapaithook in the middle, and suddenly it buckled in on itself and everything disappeared over the edge. Ofeius collapsed in anguish on the riverbank, screaming her daughter's name over and over again as she pounded the ground with her fists.

Jaywritt, who had witnessed the whole thing, ran to Shanadee screaming, "You've got to help her. You've got to help her!"

"I can't Jaywritt," she said as she held his trembling body tight against hers. She dropped to her knees on the ground and hugged him. She felt the warm tears splash on her shoulder and trickle down her back. She held him tight until his sobbing stopped. She wished he had not seen it happen. It seemed there was no escaping death. It followed them wherever they went. Just when things seemed to be going well, something else had to happen to drag them down. Poor Serondius!

Addrondett found his daughter's broken body, lying half in the water on a beach further downstream. There was no sign of the tapaithook. He brought her back to the camp in his arms and gently laid her on the ground at her mother's feet. It was the saddest thing Shanadee had ever seen. Ofeius was hysterical with grief. The river had robbed her of both her children. Now she had no one left.

The next day the band helped Ofeius and Addrondett bury their daughter in a small clearing overlooking the river. The loss deeply affected the small group and all the joy and promise had been drained from the trip. Ofeius refused to go any further and so the band had to say goodbye and continue upriver without her and Addrondett. They left her sitting by the small grave. Addrondett stood by her side with his head bowed. Neither of them looked up to watch the others leave.

There were only eight of them left.

Half their meat supply was lost with the tapaithook.

There was nothing to do but go on.

More than two weeks had passed from the time they had left until they finally arrived at the head of the Great Lake where the Great River began its journey to the sea. It was much longer than they had thought, but then things happened that they had never planned for. Lately Shanadee wondered if they should have done this, but that all changed when the trail led them out of the woods and the lake stretched out before them. The water seemed to go on forever, as far as she could see. The shoreline on both sides was dotted with wigwams. Smoke filtered lazily through the trees from many campfires. Sounds of children's laughter came from the nearest camp. Shanadee had never seen so many of her people. They were everywhere. It looked like a safe and happy place. She felt the doubt and worry fall away as she stood there with the rest of the band, staring at the scene spread out before them.

Two tapaithooks out on the lake turned and came toward them. Many of those at the nearest camp came down the shoreline to meet the small band as they stood there at the edge of the water.

Jeddilledt looked at Shanadee and smiled. "You were right Shanadee," he said as he went to help the teenagers pull the remaining tapaithook on the last leg of the trip up the river.

"Yes," said Ebanatho, "this is a good place. I think the children will be safe here."

Jaywritt and his friend had dropped their loads upon seeing the great camp spread out before them, and were immediately drawn into the group of camp children that quickly surrounded them.

Jaywritt turned and gave a quick wave to Shanadee and then ran off laughing and shouting with the group. Shanadee smiled as she watched Jaywritt racing to keep up with the rest. He will be happy here, she thought. This really is a good place.

The two tapaithooks from the lake arrived and towed the band's loaded tapaithook along the shoreline to a spot where there was enough space to build a wigwam for the group. They pulled the tapaithook onto the beach and helped unload the supplies.

That night the eight of them slept outside near their campfire. It had been a long, hard trip and they were all glad to have it behind them. Lying on her back, looking up at the canopy of bright twinkling stars, Shanadee softly hummed a Beothuk lullaby to Jaywritt, until he fell asleep with his head by her shoulder.

She lay there a long time afterward, contentedly listening to the quiet night sounds of the camp, until she finally drifted into a peaceful, dreamless sleep.

Early the next morning the men of the camp gathered together with Jeddilledt and began building a large wigwam for the band. While this was going on the women prepared a feast to welcome the newest members. Shanadee had never seen so much activity. There were people everywhere, chatting happily as they went about their work. Across the clearing two little girls laughed and shouted to each other as they chased a fluttering yellow butterfly that managed to stay just out of their reach as it weaved and danced on the wind's gentle currents. There doesn't seem to be any fear of the Buggishaman here, she thought.

The wigwam was finished by late afternoon and tribe members from other camps around the lake began arriving for the welcome feast. Eating, singing, and dancing went on late into the night. It had been a long time since Shanadee and her other band members ate without worrying whether or not they would have enough food. It was a great feeling. This makes the trip all worthwhile she thought as she watched the party going on around her.

As the night progressed, the tribe members told the newcomers their stories of how they arrived here at the Great Lake, and about their encounters with the Buggishaman on the coast. The stories were mostly the same. Most of them had lost some family members and had been forced to move inland to escape the killing. They all agreed that the Buggishaman must be avoided, and the Beothuk must become invisible.

The older tribe members told stories of days past when the Beothuk were the only people on this beautiful island. Days when there were no enemies to be avoided and they were free to roam the land in peace and safety.

They talked of how the Great Lake was now the place of the Beothuk. It was a safe place, far enough from the coast that the Buggishaman did not come here. They said it was a place where the Beothuk could once again live in peace and be happy.

As she listened to the people talk, Shanadee felt good. She felt that she was with family again. These were her people. This was going to be a good place for Jaywritt to grow. The hated Buggishaman would not bother them here.

Looking around her at all the happy smiling faces, she knew she was finally home.

Chapter 8
1796
The Newcomers

It was hard to believe so much time had passed since the eight of them had walked out of the woods down at the end of the lake. That was five years ago, but it still seemed like only yesterday. That day had changed her life, and for the better. Living here with the larger tribe made life so much easier. There were many hunters here which took a huge load off her. Hunting had become a pleasure again with the pressure of providing for the band lifted.

She now had much more time to spend with Jaywritt, and much of this time she spent teaching him the hunting skills she had learned at her father's side. He was now ten, just two years younger than she had been when her father was killed. That seemed like such a long time ago to her now, yet the memory of that terrible day had never really faded.

Jaywritt was eager to learn, just as she had been, and it was easy to see how much he loved to hunt with her. At first he had scared away more game than he had taken. That was before he learned to keep his endless questions until they were back at camp. He always told her, and anyone else who would listen, that his dream was to be as good with the hathemay as she was, and she had to admit he was getting very accurate.

Sitting cross-legged on the ground inside her wigwam, Shanadee was working on some new arrows for her and Jaywritt. She patiently wound a thin line around the shaft of one of the arrows, lashing a split goose feather to its end. This part had to be done carefully, or the arrow would not fly straight and true. Many years ago, when they started to hunt together, her father had shown her how the placement of the feathers affected the flight of an arrow. She always took extra care with this part of the construction. It could make the difference between the arrow hitting its target or missing it.

Lifting the arrow she ran her eye down the length of it. Satisfied with its straight line, she laid it on the ground next to the eight she had already finished.

The string she was using had come from a fisherman's net that had been taken from the river. It was much easier to work with than the spruce roots they had used when her father first showed her how to make arrows.

All that she had left to do was to spread a thin layer of spruce sap over the bindings. Once hardened, it would tighten the bindings and smooth the surface. Then the arrows would be ready to use.

The familiar sounds and smells of the busy camp surrounded her as she worked. The cries of happy children playing outside in the snow intermingled with the animated conversations of the women around the cooking fires. The smoke that occasionally drifted over her, swirled through the open doorway by the gentle breeze, brought with it the savory scent of cooking meat, and made her feel contented and at home. This was a good place. There was no doubt in her mind that they had made the right decision to come here. She only wished they had made the decision before.

Many other small bands had drifted in and joined the tribe at the Great Lake over the past few years. Occasionally, some of them left again to move back near the coast just to be able to fish. Always the stories were the same. The Buggishaman continued to move into their hunting grounds, pushing them away from the sea, most often with violent results. Every year there were more and more of the Buggishaman coming in from the sea in their big sailing ships. Shanadee had no idea what was out there on the other side of the sea or where all the Buggishaman were coming from. They just kept arriving, and when they did they set about building wooden houses everywhere as though they owned the land.

Although much of the snow had melted around the clearing, the air held the threat of a storm. Shanadee could smell the coldness of it through the open door. She stepped outside and looked up at the sky. Dark clouds were looming menacingly out over the lake and the wind was starting to pick up. There was no doubt a storm was headed their way. Hopefully this is the last one this winter, she thought as she wrapped the blanket a little tighter around her and went back into the wigwam. It's time for spring to be here now.

Sure enough, by the time they had eaten supper the storm hit the camp with a vengeance. The wind roared around the wigwam and threatened to rip it to shreds. The whirling snow made it impossible to see anything outside. Shanadee lashed down the door and everyone lay in their sleeping furs listening to the fury of the angry blizzard prowling around outside their door.

When Shanadee opened her eyes the next morning, she was struck by the absolute silence. The roar of the violent storm that had assailed the wigwam all night long had stopped sometime in the early morning, and had been replaced by an almost eerie stillness. The darkness had been washed away and she could see rays of bright yellow sunlight filtering through the smoke hole high in the top of the wigwam. Looking around her, Shanadee discovered that no one else was stirring. She was the only one awake. Wispy trails of smoke lazily curled into the air from the fading embers of the smoldering fire at the center of the tent, drifting up towards the clear blue sky through the opening in the roof. The wild storm had passed.

Shanadee threw some sticks on the embers to heat up the chilly wigwam. Then she knelt and untied the bottom of the door flap. She pulled it towards her and found herself looking out over the mound of fresh snow that had piled up against the outside of the door. Spread out before her was a brilliantly white, unmarked landscape. The sunlight bouncing off the surface of the snow burned her eyes, forcing her to squeeze them almost completely shut. All around the clearing the trees were covered with a heavy cloak of white, their branches bent to the ground with the weight of their load. Directly across the clearing she saw several sleds, still loaded with supplies, sitting near the door of the nearest wigwam. They had not been there all night, otherwise they would have been completely buried in snow. Someone must have arrived sometime last night in the midst of the storm.

Shanadee stepped through the door and waded into the deep snow that was well above her knees. Scooping a handful of the clean, fluffy, white snow, she held it to her tongue. The cool, tingling sensation as the snow instantly turned to water in her mouth reminded her of when she was a little girl. She smiled at the memory, and was turning to step back into her doorway when motion at the entrance of the wigwam across the clearing caught her eye. A tall young Indian she hadn't seen before, probably around her age, stepped out of the door and pushed his way through the deep snow drifts.

He had almost reached the first sled when he realized he was being watched. Turning towards Shanadee, he smiled and waved.

"Good morning," he said

Tentatively she returned the greeting. “Good morning.”

She was stricken by the gentleness in his dark eyes and suddenly she was filled with awkwardness she had never felt before. She became aware of a strange tightness in her chest and her breathing wasn’t quite right. She turned and quickly ducked back into her wigwam.

While she had been standing outside the door the others had begun stirring, and most were now fully awake and pushing out of their caribou and bear skin bed coverings. One of the women had stoked the fire in preparation for the morning meal. The others had busied themselves with rolling up the bed mats and stowing them against the walls. Jaywritt and the two young boys from the other two families sharing the wigwam were unceremoniously rolled out of their beds by one of the mothers and were given orders to bring water from the river. Shanadee watched in amusement as her brother struggled to come fully awake, shakily stood to his feet, yawned and stretched sleepily.

Her breathing felt normal again. The strange tightness in her chest had disappeared too.

Startled by the whoop of glee from the first boy through the door, Jaywritt rubbed his knuckles in his eyes and rushed through the opening after him. Shanadee picked up the water container and followed him to the door.

“Are you forgetting something?” she asked, holding out the dried caribou stomach.

With a sheepish grin, he turned, grabbed the water pouch from her, and ran back into the deep snow, yelling happily to his friends.

"It won't be long before the clearing is tramped down with those three out there," she said to Ebanatho, who was coaxing life into the fire.

"If we only had half the energy!" she replied.

"Yes, half might be enough," laughed Shanadee.

"Probably more than I can handle."

"There are newcomers in the camp," said Shanadee.

"Really? They came in last night's storm!"

"Yes. I just saw one of them outside at their sleds."

"I wonder where they came in from. It must have been hard in all that snow."

"We will soon find out I'm sure. It won't take long for that kind of news to spread."

"Now that's the truth," she laughed.

Glancing through the open doorway, Shanadee noticed the stranger was still working on the sleds. It seemed as if her eyes were drawn to him. It was the strangest feeling. Shaking her head in confusion, she moved further back into the wigwam and busied herself with helping prepare the meal. Her mind kept wandering back to those eyes. They were the most attractive she had ever seen.

Just as Shanadee predicted, by mid-morning everyone in the camp knew about the twelve newcomers who had fought their way through the wild winter blizzard to reach the camp. They said there had been fourteen of them when they left the northern part of the island a couple of weeks ago. Two of the older ones had succumbed to the freezing cold of the storm and had to be left behind.

Much of the talk around the camp was about their leader. He was a large man with a deep jagged scar that split his lip and ran diagonally across his chin, leaving him with a fierce looking face. Some of the smaller children were scared of him and hid behind their mothers when he passed by.

Shanadee knew there would be a welcome celebration tonight. It was the custom. She would find out who the stranger was then. She had been thinking of little else as she worked through the morning. She had been so occupied with thoughts of the stranger, the morning had passed without her realizing it. By the time she looked out the door again, the snow in the clearing was trampled flat as it had been before the storm. The only difference was the small banks of snow that completely ringed the camp.

That evening, Shanadee brought rabbit stew to the big rectangular wigwam that the tribe used for meetings and celebrations. As was custom, the newcomers would be served a meal by the women of the camp. This was not only a time to get to know the newcomers, but also an opportunity for the whole tribe to get together and celebrate. Everyone had packed into the large wigwam. There was no space left unoccupied. There was barely enough room to walk around. Everyone was talking and laughing at the same time. It created a festive feeling in the large tent.

Once everyone had arrived, the women began moving around the wigwam with the pots of food. The newcomers were served first, then everyone received a share. There was plenty of hot food to go around. The deafening noise created by the talking and laughter slowly subsided and was replaced with quiet slurping of the liquid stew and contented chewing of the boiled meat. Occasionally the silence was punctuated by a murmur of satisfaction; sounds of people enjoying a good meal in the presence of good company.

Looking around her, Shanadee watched the animated, happy faces of the tribe. It gave her a contented feeling to be with her people. She was standing in a corner at the back of the wigwam with a container of stew in her hands. Her eyes scanned the crowd of hungry people looking for anyone who might want a second serving. She had noticed Jaywritt, and some of the other children, had positioned themselves to be near the man with the terrible scar. She knew they were anxious to hear what had happened to his face. They are probably imaging all sorts of fierce and heroic battles he has been in, she thought. She watched as they whispered among themselves as they ate, their actions leaving no doubt as to whom they were discussing.

Shanadee's eyes were once again drawn to the young Indian sitting next to the newcomer's leader. His face was smooth and dyed a deep red. He wore his long black hair in a single braid down his back, with a bright blue feather positioned in the crown. He is good to look at, thought Shanadee.

She watched as the leader wiped out the last bit of the delicious stew with his fingers, and then placed them between his battered lips to suck the last of the tasty liquid. Smiling with satisfaction, he placed the birch bark container on the ground, rose to his feet and looked around the wigwam. His deep, powerful voice reached every corner of the large room and the tribe fell silent. Every eye turned and focused on the imposing figure he struck, standing there in the center of the wigwam. His wide, square face was framed by long, flowing, dark, shoulder length hair. His black eyes were deep in the shadows of thick bushy eyebrows, and the ugly gash in his lower lip drew his mouth down at a sharp angle on the right side.

"I am Nonosabasut," he began. "I thank you, my Beothuk brothers and sisters, for welcoming us here," he continued, sweeping his hand in a wide circle around the room and bowing his head in a show of respect.

After a moment he lifted his head and continued, "We have travelled far to find more of our people. We were told there were many Beothuks at the Great Lake. It is good to see it is so."

A murmur of acknowledgement rippled through the wigwam.

"It is no longer safe to live by the sea," he continued in his deep rumbling voice. "The Buggishaman does not want to live side by side with the Beothuk. He only wants to kill us and take everything that we have. This beautiful land of our ancestors gives us enough for everyone, but he does not want to share. Our spears and our hathemay and arrows cannot fight their guns. We can only survive in larger numbers. It is no longer safe to be alone in small bands. That is why we left the coast behind to join you here at the Great Lake."

Many of those seated around the room nodded in agreement with his words.

Jaywritt, and the group of young boys sitting in the front, had to tilt their heads way back to look at the tall giant standing in front of them. They sat motionless, with their mouths wide open, in anticipation of what he would say next.

Nonosabasut's hand involuntarily rubbed the pink scar on his chin as he talked. "We have other enemies up there in the north as well," he said. "They cross the ice from the frozen land. They come to fish in our waters. That's how this came to be," he rumbled in his deep, gentle voice, looking down at the boys. "They raided our village on the coast. A great battle followed. I was struck down with a hatchet. Many of our people died that day. Many of their people died too."

The young boys, who had been hanging on his every word, seemed to breathe out as one as though they had been collectively holding their breath. They continued watching the stranger with awe, not daring to look away in case they would miss something he said.

Shanadee smiled at her ten year old brother. She knew he would be talking nonstop about this man for the next few days. It would be hard for him to get to sleep after listening to this. His vivid imagination would be running wild, controlling his every waking moment.

Nonosabasut went on to introduce each of the other eleven members of the group, ending with the man Shanadee had been watching all night. "This is my brother Kirradittii," he said affectionately. "He killed the one who did this to me before he could take the second blow. He saved my life that day. I owe him everything," he said laying his large hand on his brother's shoulder.

The tent erupted in applause as he announced this.

Kirradittii's eyes swept around the tent, acknowledging those present with a shy nod. When he found her in the group of women standing along the back, his eyes lingered and he smiled in recognition. Shanadee met his gaze and held it this time until his eyes moved on. Her insides were doing a strange but wonderful dance, and once again she found it hard to breathe.

Feeling a nudge at her back, she turned to find one of the young women grinning broadly at her. "He saw you, Shanadee."

Shanadee sheepishly dropped her eyes and playfully pushed her away. He had noticed her, she thought, as she gathered up her containers and headed back to her wigwam. The large, round moon overhead smiled down at her, reflecting off the snow, making the night almost as bright as day. Little clouds of moisture hung all around her head as she expelled her hot breath into the quiet night air.

"He really did notice me!" she said aloud with a girlish giggle. Self-consciously she looked around to make sure she was alone.

Spring arrived quickly. It seemed that one day you were wading through snow as high as your waist, and the next it had melted and disappeared into the ground. The swollen rivers and ponds soon returned to normal, and summer hurried its way towards winter. The busy days quickly rushed by. There was always something to be done to prepare for the next season. The cycle never changed much.

Shanadee's encounters with Kirradittii grew more and more frequent. There always seemed to be a reason for them to be in the same place at the same time. She looked forward in anticipation to those times and did her best to find ways to make them happen. She thought maybe Kirradittii was doing the same.

Shanadee sometimes caught other women exchanging knowing glances when she and Kirradittii were around each other. Although she brushed it off as meddling women's nosiness, inwardly she loved the fact that she was the one with him and not any of them. Once in a while she even went out of her way to flaunt it in their faces. There was a certain satisfaction in it, and though it didn't last it was always fun!

During that summer, Nonosabasut became the tribal chief. From the first day the tribe had recognized that he was a born leader, and the role just seemed to fall naturally on his broad shoulders. Although there was no formal council to appoint or elect him, the tribe members found themselves seeking his guidance on matters involving the daily life at the Great Lake. His powerful external strength was balanced by a gentle spirit that often brought a calming influence to disputes. Shanadee found that behind that terribly scarred face there was a kind and caring man; one who loved his brother dearly.

Although every effort was made to avoid contact with the Buggishaman, excursions to the coast were still undertaken from time to time during the summer. These were carefully planned and even more carefully executed. Only under cover of fog would they risk paddling out to the Bird Islands where they could harvest supplies of eggs and birds. These boat trips were always taken from secluded and yet uninhabited coves, places where the Buggishaman had not yet staked a claim.

Whenever there was opportunity, and they were sure the Buggishaman was not around, they took metal objects from the fishermen's sheds and boats to fashion into arrowheads or other tools. They also made it a point to replenish their odemet supply when they made those trips to the coast.

Although great care was taken to avoid contact, these trips were not always without incident. Usually they travelled in larger groups to get to the coast, but once there they often split into smaller groups to get the work done. More than once Shanadee listened to the stories of those who returned without some members of their party. Most times the missing people were never found because they couldn't risk spending time at the coast searching for them.

Every year during the late spring, many of the tribe would leave the large camp at the Great Lake and move to other parts of the island in search of food supplies. Then as the fall season approached, they would begin to trickle back and the community at the Lake would grow quickly again.

After arriving at the Great Lake, Shanadee had never returned to the coast. She did not want to take the trip until Jaywritt was older and could take care of himself. It was too risky and she had already lost the rest of her family there. For now she was content to stay at the lake.

Kirradittii did not share her feelings on this. He had left mid-summer, with a group of men, to travel down the river to the ocean. They left in three large tapaithooks, planning to return before winter with fish and birds to replenish the camp supplies. Standing in front of the open door of her wigwam that day, Shanadee had watched as Nonosabasut hugged his younger brother, waited for him to get in the last tapaithook and then pushed them off from the shore. She returned Kirradittii's wave and then anxiously watched them until they disappeared around the bend in the river. She had an uneasy feeling that she might not see him again, and it made her very scared.

Never once, during that long summer, did she look out her door without glancing down the lake towards the mouth of the river. As the days slowly passed, and the forest slopes turned from green to brilliant red and gold, she grew more and more anxious. Often she would sit on the grassy bank of the lake facing towards the river mouth while she hammered out pieces of metal, forming them into arrow heads. As she worked, her eyes kept drifting back to where she had last seen his tall straight back and bright blue feather as the last tapaithook had left the lake and entered the river. She hoped he was safe. Many times she asked the Great Spirit to protect him and bring him back to her.

Many of the long summer evenings after her work was done, she spent with Jaywritt as he practiced with the short hathemay. She was a demanding teacher, and his shoulders would often ache from the repeated shooting. Again and again she would have him shoot arrows at targets she had paced out in the clearing, until she satisfied herself that he could place an arrow wherever she asked him to. She had him practice in quiet windless conditions as well as on windy days to show him how changes in the weather affected the arrows path.

Shanadee took him on hunting trips with her, and taught him how to track and stalk animals just the way she had learned at their father's side. She told him stories of her hunting trips with their father, Nanolute. She talked with him about their mother, Manddilleeitt, and his older brother, Timmwall. Jaywritt had been so young when they died. She wanted to keep their names and their memory alive.

The warmth had seeped out of the days, and the nights had grown chilly. Winter was subtly announcing it's soon arrival. The group at the Lake was busy preparing their food stores and repairing the wigwams in anticipation of another cold Newfoundland winter.

The late fall chill had crept into the wigwam overnight while they were sleeping. Lying there in the warmth of the heavy bearskin blanket, Shanadee watched her breath float towards the ceiling as she softly blew it into the cool air. Reluctantly she pushed back the warm blanket, crawled through the early morning gloom past the sleeping form of her brother, and stoked the smoldering fire embers into a warm blaze. She sat there feeding the fire until she could feel the warmth begin to spread out through the room. Then she moved to the door, pushed back the animal skin, and peered outside. The Lake was lightly frozen, with a skim of dark thin ice that rippled with the movement of the water underneath. As was her usual custom, she glanced down toward the mouth of the river, and her breath caught as she saw tapaithooks moving into the Lake in the distance. One, two, and three she counted. They were all there! They had returned!

Ducking back inside, she hurriedly grabbed a blanket from the floor, swung it over her shoulders and wrapped it tight around herself. She stepped through the door and quickly walked to the shoreline of the lake. There, she was joined by others who had also spotted the group down at the end of the lake. Soon the whole camp was drawn by the noisy, excited group at the shoreline. Nonosabasut, who was standing in the center of the group, towered over the others.

Shanadee's worry that they might not all be there was short lived. As they drew nearer she spotted the blue feather on that familiar head at the front of the lead tapaithook. A smile crept across her face in anticipation. He was back! She couldn't wait to look into those dark eyes. She stood a little behind Nonosabasut, impatiently waiting for the boat to reach the shore.

As soon as the bow of the boat scraped the soft sand of the shoreline, Kirradittii leaped over the side of the lead tapaithook, splashed through the shallow water to his brother and embraced him in a bear hug. All around them the others found their relatives, and hugged and kissed them happily. Finally, after what seemed an eternity to Shanadee, he disengaged himself from his brother's powerful arms and turned to her. He wrapped his arms around her waist, lifted her off the ground and held her tight against him in a lingering hug.

Breathlessly she said, "I missed you Kirradittii," as she smiled up at the face she had been eagerly watching for all summer.

"I missed you too Shanadee. I thought of you, every day." He held her at arm's length and smiled at her with those beautiful eyes. Her stomach muscles fluttered.

Shanadee couldn't remember when she had felt so happy.

"We will talk later", he said. "I have to help unload the boats now."

Reluctantly she released him and stood there has he walked back to the tapaithooks. She felt that she never wanted to let him out of her sight again. Not since she was twelve years old had she anyone in her life who could make her feel safe, nor had there been anyone who she could talk to as she could to this man. She knew he was the one who could fill the emptiness and take away the loneliness that had invaded her heart after she had lost her family.

As she stood there watching it soon became apparent they had had a very successful trip. They unloaded; fish, monau, shellfish, eggs, and birds from the tapaithooks. They had containers of ochre, containers of iron pieces, several hatchets, and a large sail. They also had two buckets filled with potatoes. All of this was carried up to the storage house, sorted and put away.

Later that evening, just before the sun went down, everyone gathered in the large wigwam to celebrate their safe return and to hear the men tell their stories about what they had seen and what had happened to them on their trip down to the coast.

Shanadee sat next to Jaywritt on the hard packed ground, with her back against a wall.

"Did you see all the eggs and birds they brought back?"

"Yes little brother, I did," she smiled at him.

"How did they get so many? And don't call me little brother!"

Shanadee was about to answer when she was interrupted by one of the older men who had stood to his feet.

"This was one of the best trips I have ever been on," he announced. "It was like the old days, when I was younger."

"Well that wasn't yesterday!" someone in the group shouted.

Playfully shaking his fist at the speaker, he raised his voice over the laughter and continued. "The first thing we did when we got to the coast was to take two of the tapaithooks out to the bird islands. Kirradittii and some of the other men stayed on shore to gather shellfish while we were gone."

The mention of his name perked Shanadee's interest and her eyes scanned those sitting near the fire, coming to rest on the long braid with the telltale blue bird feather. At first she thought she had picked a bad seat, but then she realized she had a better seat. I can watch him and he can't see me, she thought.

"We paddled out of the bay in darkness, before the sun came up. There was no fog to hide us so we had to leave in the dark," continued the storyteller.

"Did the Buggishaman see you?" came from somewhere in the crowd.

"No. No one saw us. We were very careful. We left from a cove where the Buggishaman has no buildings."

A second man pushed to his feet, placed his arm across the old man's shoulder and joined in the story. "It took almost two hours of paddling to reach the islands", he said. "The waves were very big. Sometimes we could not see the other tapaithook as we went down the other side of the wave. For a while we could not see land anywhere… just water everywhere."

An audible murmur rippled through the crowd, like a small wave breaking on the beach.

"As we got closer, we could see a great cloud of birds over the small island. There was so many that sometimes the sun couldn't shine through."

"Wow," said one of the small boys sitting near the front. Like the rest of his friends he was sitting cross legged on the ground staring up at the storytellers, eyes huge with wonder.

Spurred on by his responsive audience, the new storyteller continued. "The island was covered with birds," he said sweeping his arms wide around the room. "Nests were everywhere. You could not walk without stepping on one," he said, dramatically high stepping around the fire for the benefit of the boys. "When we began gathering the eggs the air was filled with screeching angry birds."

"Did they attack?" asked one of the boys, incredulously.

"They sure did. They dove and swooped at our heads," he replied weaving and diving in front of his captive audience.

"Did they bite you?" asked one of the little girls timidly.

"No," he laughed. "They just tried to scare us away from their nests. We knocked some of them out of the air with clubs. We could have filled the two tapaithooks with eggs, but we could not use them all. We only took what we needed. We also took many birds as well."

"You were a brave Indian," teased one of his companions.

Ignoring the taunt, he enthusiastically picked up the story again. "We filled one tapaithook and towed it with the other, so there were five of us in one tapaithook. We had to be really careful not to tip the tapaithook," he said, swaying as if in the rolling tapaithook. "It would have been a long swim," he laughed, and slapped his fellow storyteller on the back.

"Further than you can swim," laughed the other.

Around the room pockets of laughter and clapping broke out in response.

The third man now stood and began to speak. "It was later in the evening when we returned to the bay from where we left, probably about an hour before dark. When we were paddling into the bay we paddled into a school of herring. The water was alive with them. They were breaking the surface like rain. A bunch of harbor monau were feeding on them and driving them into the bay toward the beach. We speared three of the monau before we reached the beach.

"When we got ashore we hid the birds, the eggs, and the three monau in a cave until we were ready to prepare them to come back up river. We had a fine feed of monau that night."

To Shanadee's delight, Kirradittii began talking next. Unlike his brother, he stood at just over five feet tall. His face was smooth and he wore his hair in a long braid down his back. Sticking out horizontally, from the top of the braid, was a bright blue feather from a blue jay. He wore leggings, dyed a deep red, and, like most of the younger men, was bare from the waist up.

Shanadee watched the muscles ripple across his back as he pushed himself up from his sitting position. The summer trip had done him good. He was looking good!

She noticed how the other men looked at him as he rose to speak. It was obvious to her that he had gained their respect on the trip. Glancing at Nonosabasut she saw he had the beginnings of a faint smile on his face as well. She knew that it was his pride pushing to the surface.

Kirradittii began to speak. "A few days later we hid in the woods around a small village and watched the Buggishaman. They were loading a big sailing boat with dried fish. They worked all day long to get it finished. When the sun went down some of us sneaked under the wharf in one of our tapaithooks."

Shanadee noticed she was not the only one listening intently to Kirradittii speak. The whole room was leaning toward him in anticipation. She smiled happily to herself.

"It's nice to see you smiling so much again sister."

"I'm very happy, Jaywritt," she whispered softly.

"I know."

"We were really careful not to make a sound," Kirradittii continued, lowering his voice just above a whisper. "Everyone left the wharf but one Buggishaman. He was the man who had been telling the others what do all day. He stood on the wharf, just above us, watching the boat for a long, long time. We sat there quietly waiting. We waited until the moon was at the top of the sky. Then, finally, the last Buggishaman left. We watched until the lights went out in his cabin."

Around the room little murmurs of appreciation could be heard at what they expected to hear him say next. Everyone was leaning toward him, straining to hear.

"We cut the lines that tied the boat to the wharf and then we dragged the boat out of the harbor, with our tapaithook. We pulled the boat into another bay. There, we let the waves push it up onto the rocks."

"Tell us what was in the boat," shouted someone.

"Yes. Tell us."

Kirradittii nodded in the direction of the sound, and said, "Inside the boat, we found iron to use for arrows. We found pots and hatchets and guns. We broke the guns into pieces and threw them in the water. Then we cut down the sails. Some of the things we hid in the woods to get later. It was too much for our tapaithooks to carry."

Someone began to clap in excitement. Soon the whole room had erupted in shouts of joy and praise for the great and brave deed.

"I will be going on the next trip," Jaywritt announced at her side.

Shanadee felt a small chill of fear wash over her. He was the only family she had left, but he would be eleven soon. She knew that was probably old enough, but how could she let him go. Not wanting to embarrass him, she smiled and nodded to him, hoping he could not see the worry on her face. Anyway there would be a whole year pass by before the next trip would happen.

"Wait. There is more," shouted Kirradittii, as he raised his hands to silence the crowd. Smiling, he turned and nodded to the man who sat on the ground next to him and then he sat down.

The fourth man stood to take his turn and said, "We had begun our return trip and we were paddling up the river when we came around a bend and surprised a family of settlers in a field. They were pulling potatoes from the ground. When they saw us, they all ran to their wooden house. They left three buckets filled with potatoes. The buckets were just sitting there in the field where they dropped them when they ran."

"We quickly paddled our tapaithook to the shore. I jumped out, ran into the field, and grabbed two of the buckets. Suddenly, the Buggishaman burst out of the house with a gun. Boom," shouted the storyteller, as he smacked his hands together in emphasis.

Laughter trickled through the adults as the young boys jumped with fright.

Taking the cue from his audience the storyteller became more animated. "He shot at me and the third bucket exploded into a shower of potatoes," he said waving his arms in the air. "I doubled over," he said bending low to the ground to demonstrate, "and raced back to the tapaithook with the other two buckets, spilling potatoes as I ran."

"What happened then?"

"The others shot arrows at the Buggishaman from the beach."

"Did he shoot his gun again?"

"No. He ran back into the house. We did not see him again. We quickly paddled away from there," he said, and sat back down on the ground, laughing with the others.

Again the room erupted into excited clapping and shouting. The excitement was infectious. The whole camp was energized by the group's good fortune and the fact that all had returned unharmed, despite the close encounter with the Buggishaman. The men were praised for their bravery, and their boldness in the face of the Buggishaman's gun. They sang and danced in celebration well into the early morning hours.

Knowing Kirradittii was safely back in camp made Shanadee feel happy once more. Her heart had swelled with pride, and she had not taken her eyes off him while he was telling his story. A warm feeling had spread through her chest. She felt an overpowering need to be near him, to feel his breath on her face. A little shiver of delight rippled through her body. She liked this feeling. This was a *good* feeling.

Chapter 9
1798
KIRRADITTII

Jaywritt had grown to be a strong young man in the last 9 years. He had thrived under the watchful eye of his sister. At twelve, he was now just one year younger than Shanadee had been that dreadful day when the Buggishaman had killed their mother and brother. She remembered how that day she had wondered how long she and Jaywritt would survive, and here they were doing fine. Shanadee watched proudly as he slipped his long hathemay over his shoulder and joined the small hunting party heading up the lake to find caribou. She had taught him everything she knew about hunting, and she knew he was ready. They had practiced for hours with the hathemay until he could place his arrow within inches of hers with every shot.

As she watched the boys disappear around a bend further up the lake, she became aware of someone standing behind her. Without turning she knew it was Kirradittii. They had grown much closer since he came back from his trip to the coast. She always felt better when he was nearby. He was a good hunter and he had brought plenty of meat to the camp since they had moved inland to the Great Lake.

Most of the tribe had moved away from the coast and now lived around the lake. In all there were more than 70 tribe members here. That was not as many as there had been when she had originally come to the Great Lake, but it was still a large group.

Kirradittii lived with his brother' Nonosabasut, at the main camp closest to the mouth of the river. It was the same camp in which Shanadee and Jaywritt lived.

"I see you, Shanadee," he said, as he moved closer to the shoreline where she was standing looking out over the glassy surface of the lake. Here and there the surface was momentarily darkened as the wind directed its light breath toward the water, and small rings rippled from the spot where a trout leaped in pursuit of tiny insects, but otherwise the lake lay quiet and undisturbed.

"I see you, Kirradittii," she replied softly without turning.

"Your brother has grown well. He is a good hunter," smiled Kirradittii.

"He is like my father," replied Shanadee, as she thoughtfully stared up the lake where she had watched Jaywritt walk into the forest.

"They say you are the best marksman in the camp. Perhaps he is more like you than he is like his father."

"Perhaps he is."

"I would like to hunt with you someday. I would like to see you shoot. I want to see if you are as good as they say you are."

Hearing the playful challenge in his voice, Shanadee replied, "How about now, Kirradittii?" Turning quickly on her heel, she strode past him with a taunting grin and disappeared inside her wigwam. In moments she reappeared at the door with her long hunting hathemay over her shoulder and a leather quiver of arrows at her side. With a mischievous glance at Kirradittii, she stepped through the doorway and headed into the woods away from the lake.

Soundlessly, Kirradittii jogged up the path behind her and settled in, a pace or so behind her. He felt no need to be the leader. Today he was content to follow. All he wanted to do was watch her hunt. He intended to enjoy this trip.

A lot of things had changed since he and his brother had come to the Great Lake. Probably the best was the beautiful creature gliding silently up the path ahead of him. Before the Lake they had lived in constant fear of attack from the Buggishaman or the people from the frozen land. There was no peace, and they had to always be on the alert for enemies, ready to do battle. Life here was so different. Here his hathemay was only needed to hunt food, not to kill other men. He hoped he would never have to do that again. If he could capture Shanadee's heart and live in peace for the rest of his life he would be a very happy man.

They walked in silence until the path came out on the top of a small hill where they could look out over the camp stretching along the banks of the huge lake. Thin, wispy trails of smoke drifted lazily into the still morning air, spiraling out of the openings at the tops of the wigwams. They were already too far away to hear the camp sounds clearly, but in the distance they could see the smaller children running and playing in the clearing they had just left. Out on the silvery lake a lone tapaithook moved slowly along the far shoreline. Standing there, looking at the peaceful scene, Shanadee thought of her younger days; a time when her family was complete and happy; a time before the hated Buggishaman had so violently pushed his way into her life. She wondered if she would have a time like that again. Maybe with this man, she thought. Maybe life *will* get better.

As if somehow sensing her thoughts, Kirradittii reached out and placed his hand on her bare shoulder. She felt something hot flowing through her body beneath the skin. His touch had triggered a feeling stronger than she had ever felt before. It was as if something were physically drawing her to this man. A tiny tremor coursed through her body, and she stepped back in confusion.

"Let's go," she said.

Without looking back at him she turned, ran down the gentle slope, and veered off the path into the woods. With satisfaction she sensed he was keeping pace with her, although he was so quiet she had to concentrate to pick up any sound at all.

While on the hill top she had spotted caribou crossing a bog in the distance. She was taking a line through the woods that would bring her to the edge of the bog, directly in their path. With her hathemay now in her left hand she ran swiftly, hopping lightly over downed trees and windfall debris that lay in her path.

As she neared the bog, she slowed and waited for him to catch up. She noticed with pleasure that he wasn't as fast as her, but his breathing was still even and regular.

Peering out through the low brush that ringed the edge of the bog, she could see the two caribou still walking in their direction. The lead bull stopped occasionally, raised his head and sniffed the air, testing it for danger. The large rack adorning his head gleamed white in the bright sunlight. Behind him the smaller cow grazed contentedly, totally relying on him for their safety.

Kirradittii noticed how Shanadee had cleverly placed herself so that if the animals stayed on their current path they would pass well within her arrow range. The place she had picked to hide was downwind from the caribou, so there was no chance of the animals picking up their scent.

Shanadee slipped her arms out of her restricting tunic and let it slip to her waist, freeing her arms to shoot.

She notched one arrow and held a second between the fingers of her lead hand.

She stood motionless.

Her breathing was normal.

She waited patiently.

Kirradittii knelt on the ground to her right. He did not raise his hathemay. He watched her stance with admiration, enjoying the fine smooth curves of her upper body. He found it hard to move his eyes from her to the approaching caribou. Seeing her this way for the first time was making him a little lightheaded. He had known for a long time that he wanted her, but never as much as he did right now. He forgot all about the caribou.

The two animals steadily advanced on their position, unaware of the waiting hunters. Shanadee had picked the perfect spot. When the bull entered her range of fire, she slowly pulled the hathemay string taunt, careful not to make any sudden movements. At the last second she clicked her tongue, and as the bull jerked his head up, snorting in alarm, the first arrow was in flight. The second arrow pierced his pounding heart, inches from the first. Instinctively the caribou leaped in the air and wheeled back the way it had come. It ran a few steps and stumbled to its knees, grunting in agony.

Shanadee covered the distance in seconds holding her knife in her hand. Before Kirradittii reached her, she had dispensed the animal, and was preparing to clean and carve it, to make it ready to carry back to camp.

"That was good shooting," he laughed, with open admiration in his voice.

Shanadee smiled at him. "Think you can beat that," she teased playfully.

Still laughing, he raised his hands in surrender. "No," he said, "Never! I would not even try!"

Shanadee liked the way he laughed. It sounded so free and effortless. It made her feel happy.

Lifting the front leg, Shanadee inserted the knife, and sliced open the belly of the big animal, letting the insides spill out on the ground. The air around them was immediately filled with the hot, moist, meaty smell released from the steaming cavity.

Kirradittii unconsciously licked his lips as the juices began to flow inside his mouth.

Reaching into the chest, Shanadee pulled the heart free of the two arrows that had penetrated it and set it aside. Then she sliced off a piece of the warm slippery liver and handed it to Kirradittii. Sitting side by side on the fallen animal, they ate the liver just as their ancestors had always done, celebrating the caribou's life, and giving thanks to the Great Spirit for the gift that would feed the camp tonight.

Across the bog, Shanadee noticed the gray moisamadrook, standing in the shadows at the edge of the woods. She had not seen him for nine years, not since the day she had buried her mother and Timmwall. He must be here to tell me something, she thought. Next to her she felt Kirradittii's body stiffen as he too saw the moisamadrook. She reached out her hand to stop him as he lifted his hathemay from the ground at his feet.

"No," she whispered. "He is no threat to us. It is my father's spirit. He has come to visit me."

"How do you know?"

"I know his eyes."

"Do you see him often?" he asked, slowly lowering his hathemay.

"Only when there are big events in my life," she replied, without moving her eyes from the moisamadrook. "The last time was when my mother and my brother Timmwall died."

"So, what's the big event now?"

"Probably you," she said thoughtfully.

Kirradittii looked at her with a mixture of curiosity and surprise.

Reaching around behind her, he slipped his hand through her long hair and pulled her face to his. Feeling no resistance, he touched his lips against hers, savoring her taste mixed with the salty taste of blood from the fresh liver. His nostrils filled with her scent for the first time. His heart pounded like a dance drum as he felt the softness of her body pressing and molding to his bare chest. The sensation coursing through him was new, yet somehow familiar. Instinct told him he had found his mate.

Pushing back, he looked into her dark eyes and saw confirmation there. Aloud, he said, "Shanadee, I want you to be my wife."

Shanadee smiled into his eyes and nodded. "I would love that," she replied.

"Then I will ask my brother to arrange it," he said happily and covered her lips once again with his.

Chapter 10
1800
SHANAWDITHIT

When they got married two years ago, Kirradittii took Shanadee and her brother Jaywritt to live with him in Nonosabasut's wigwam. Shanadee remembered what it had looked like the day she moved in. She had given the place the woman's touch it had so desperately needed. The cleanly swept floor and orderly racks bore witness to her presence.

It seemed that marriage had triggered this need to be neat and organized. Maybe she just wanted to do it for Kirradittii, she didn't know, but it was something she hadn't paid a whole lot of attention to before. She wasn't even sure he really appreciated all her fussing, but he seemed to be good about it. Come to think of it, most of the time he just got out of her way when she was in a cleaning mood. He's a good man, a smart man, she thought.

"Today, my husband, you will become a father," Shanadee whispered softly in Kirradittii's ear, as he lay in the dark next to her.

Without opening his eyes, he reached his arm across the large mound of her stomach, gently pulled her close and sleepily murmured, "Then today will be a good day my little one."

Kirradittii had looked forward to this day in excited anticipation for a long time. He loved the idea of being a father. The thought of holding the tiny baby that he and Shanadee had created was always the topic of conversation. The idea that this new little person would have part of both of them intrigued him. His bubbling enthusiasm served to brighten the days at the camp. People smiled knowingly as he approached. He acted as though he was the first one to ever have a baby.

To Kirradittii this whole process was taking much too long. It seemed to be going on forever. It seemed that the day would never come.

The significance of what Shanadee had just whispered finally penetrated his sleep fogged mind and he leaped to his feet, bouncing his head off a side pole. "Hey, get up," he called to his brother and Jaywritt as he vigorously rubbed the side of his head. "We have to leave the tent to Shanadee. She is going to have the baby. Let's go! Let's go!" he said urgently.

To Shanadee he said, "I will go and get help."

Scrambling out of the door into the pre-dawn darkness, he rushed off in search of Minnoolee, the tribe's midwife. As he raced through the clearing he was yelling at the top of his lungs. "Shanadee is having the baby! She's having it now!"

Minnoolee lived in a camp further up the lake, about a ten minute walk from the main camp. Kirradittii ran along the worn path in the darkness, his mind overflowing with thoughts of what was about to happen. All he knew was he would soon see his baby for the first time.

As he broke out of the woods in the next clearing, he began shouting.

"Minnoolee. Minnoolee! Come quick old woman. Shanadee is having the baby."

Without a doubt he was waking everyone in that camp as well. He just didn't care. This was the biggest day of his life. Why should anyone sleep through this?

Minnoolee and her husband lived in the wigwam at the furthest end of the clearing. Without hesitation, Kirradittii burst through the door still shouting, "Minnoolee!" as he tried to catch his breath. "We need you. Now!"

Hearing the earlier commotion, Minnoolee had already gathered up her bag and was preparing to leave.

"Stop that yelling, son," she said. "There is lots of time."

"Hurry," said Kirradittii breathlessly. "You have to come now. You need to hurry!"

"Your baby will get here when it is ready," she replied calmly.

"But Shanadee said it will be today, he said anxiously."

"Then today you will become a father. Today you will hold your baby," she smiled at him.

Kirradittii pushed out the door in front of her, and impatiently held the flap open.

"Let's go Minnoolee," he said, gripping her arm to help her along the path. He lifted her bag from her shoulder, slung it over his, and tried his best to hurry her across the clearing towards the path.

The day had crept upon them while he was in the tent, and it was a lot easier to walk the path in the early dawn light. Still, the journey back took much longer than he had taken to get to Minnoolee's camp in the first place.

Minnoolee strolled along at a pace befitting her age and, try as he might, Kirradittii could not move her any faster. She kept up a continuous chatter as he helped her around rocks and boulders that forced the path to zigzag through the heavy forest. Her mindless prattle was driving him crazy. He just wanted to get back to Shanadee. He didn't care about what she cooked for last night's supper, nor was he interested in her husband's back problems. He just wanted her to hurry.

By the time they reached the main camp he was in a high state of agitation, mixed with a healthy dose of excitement.

Looking across the clearing, he could see Nonosabasut and Jaywritt hovering just outside the door of the wigwam. Several of the women of the tribe had gathered around waiting for old Minnoolee to arrive with her potions and take charge.

"Is everything all right?" he called across the clearing to his brother.

Nonosabasut nodded, "Shanadee is fine."

At the door of the wigwam, Minnoolee placed her hand on Kirradittii's chest and stopped him from entering.

"You wait over there," she said pointing to the grassy bank that ran up to the edge of the lake. "I will take care of your wife and your child."

Relieved, Kirradittii headed off in the direction of the lake with the other two men trailing close behind him. Minnoolee disappeared through the doorway and the caribou skin fell back into place.

The three had just stepped off the grass onto the sandy beach when the first scream froze Kirradittii in his tracks. Icy fingers of fear crawled up his back and squeezed tightly around his chest.

"Shanadee," he yelled, as he whirled around in the soft sand and started to run back. He had only made one step when he was brought up short by Nonosabasut's huge restraining hand which was now locked tightly around his arm.

"It will be alright, brother," he rumbled in his deep gentle voice. "Minnoolee will take good care of her."

"They're killing her! Can't you hear?"

"No Kirradittii. It's your child entering this world."

"I can't take it, Nonosabasut. She's in pain. I've never heard her scream like that before."

The scream stopped and the silence became deafening. Moments passed, and then the second scream rushed at him across the clearing, washing over him like a cresting wave. With a gasp, he slumped down on the sand and covered his face with his hands. The other two men sat beside him, watching his body flinch at each successive scream.

The sun slowly traveled across the sky, painting the glistening ripples on the surface of the lake a gold and silver spray. Kirradittii sat in the sand waiting, his body tensed like a fully drawn hathemay string.

A new sound suddenly rang out, breaking the latest silence. The shrill cry of a newborn brought him to his feet again. Halfway across the clearing, he stopped as the wigwam door flap was pushed aside and Minnoolee stepped into the sunlight with a bundle in her arms.

Kirradittii's eyes were fixed on the bundle. A tiny arm waved a circle in the air above the blanket and he expelled the breath he had been holding with an explosive gasp. His face was split with a boyish grin as he hurried toward them.

"Kirradittii, come take your daughter," said Minnoolee.

Kirradittii covered the remaining distance with his arms extended. As he retrieved the squirming baby from Minnoolee's arms, he looked into the old woman's eyes questioningly.

"Shanadee needs me," was her only response as she turned and hurried back into the wigwam.

Standing there, Kirradittii pulled the bundle tighter against his pounding chest and looked down into the most beautiful brown eyes he had ever seen. It was as though Shanadee's eyes had been taken and given to the little one who was returning his gaze.

"Hello little princess," he said, as he lifted her to the upright position. "You shall be known as Shanawdithit; for I can see in your eyes you have your mothers fighting spirit,"

Turning back to the two men standing nearby, he said, "Come, see your niece."

Grinning with unrestrained pleasure, the two crowded in on Kirradittii and the new child. They were so absorbed in the tiny new life that Minnoolee had to repeat herself and raise her voice. "Kirradittii, Shanadee is asking for you."

Kirradittii turned and strode into the wigwam, holding Shanawdithit tightly in his arms. The two women, who were kneeling on either side of Shanadee, gathered up the bloody blankets and went outside to join Minnoolee. Kirradittii had never seen so much blood. The air was oppressive with the strong scents of the birth. Kirradittii nervously approached the motionless figure on the ground.

Shanadee turned her head toward him, and weakly smiled. "Hello, my husband," she murmured in a thick, pain filled voice.

Kirradittii knelt on the ground near her head and held up the squirming baby.

"See what we have done," he whispered, as tears of joy trickled from the corners of his eyes. "You have given me the greatest gift of all."

Gently he laid the little one across her chest and sat on the ground watching Shanadee as she stroked Shanawdithit's short, coal black hair in amazement.

The three women reentered the wigwam. "She must rest," said Minnoolee. "We will stay with them through the night. You sleep outside," she said, as she shooed him out the door.

Thus began a week of restless pacing for Kirradittii. By the second day, Nonosabasut and Jaywritt could no longer watch the agony on Kirradittii's worried face, so they set off into the woods on a hunting trip to get fresh food.

This had to be the longest week of Kirradittii's life. He never ventured far from the wigwam, always staying within earshot. Anxiously, he watched the goings and comings of the three women and strained to hear the whispered murmurs from inside the tent. He knew Shanadee was dangerously weak and he felt helpless knowing there was nothing he could do to help. He had no choice but to leave it to Minnoolee to make her well again. But what if she couldn't? He would never be able to go on without her.

Little Shanawdithit had been given to another new mother in the tribe to nurse until Shanadee was well enough to do it herself. Each day, Kirradittii took some time from pacing in front of the wigwam and cradled his little daughter in his arms. Those were happy times, times when some of the load of worry for Shanadee was lifted from his shoulders. Looking into the baby's dark twinkling eyes, he saw her mother staring back at him. It made him smile, and strangely the love that he thought he would know only with Shanadee was mysteriously expanding to include this little one as well. He knew there was nothing he would not do to protect her.

On the sixth day Minnoolee came for him again. "You can go in now," she said.

"Has she recovered?" he asked worriedly.

"Yes, she has. I will get Shanawdithit."

"Thank you, old woman. I will always remember you for this."

"Go now," she smiled.

Kirradittii pulled aside the flap, and stepped into the wigwam. Shanadee was propped in a sitting position against a side post. The first thing he noticed was that the familiar twinkle had returned to her eyes. She looked so much better he thought with relief. He sat on the ground in front of her as Minnoolee entered with Shanawdithit wrapped in a blanket. She placed her in Shanadee's outstretched arms. "You are a family again," she said, then turned and ducked out through the door.

Chapter 11
1809
The Scar

Their third child was born two summers ago, shortly after the last snow had melted away. Shanadee and Kirradittii named him Ojjbawitt. His four year old sister, Mandolee, who had been named for her grandmother, and Shanawdithit completed their family unit.

Shanadee could not have been happier. There had been a time when she would not have dared to dream life would turn out this way. Her only regret was that her mother and father were not here to see their grandchildren. She knew they would have been so proud of them.

Many nights Shanadee and Kirradittii would sit around the cooking fire in their wigwam and tell the stories of their ancestors until the children fell asleep. They were stories that had been passed down from generation to generation, and told around cooking fires just like theirs down through the years. This kept the memories strong and taught the children to respect the customs of their people.

Shanadee talked to them about her father, Nanolute, and how he taught her to hunt and to shoot. She told of the many hunting trips they had taken together, and how he always did things to make her laugh. She told them how he taught her to respect the animals they hunted and how they gave thanks to the Great Spirit for providing them with the animals. Often, when she described the way he was taken from her by the Buggishaman that day on the ice, a tear would trickle down her cheek.

No matter how many times she heard the story, it still made Shanawdithit feel sad every time she heard her mother repeat it. She wished she could have known this man who her mother loved so much. She had never known any of her grandparents.

Other times Shanadee described the dreadful day her mother, brother and uncle were murdered by the Buggishaman. Through the telling and retelling of her stories, she taught her children to hate and fear the Buggishaman just as she did. She always told them to stay far away from them.

Their uncle, Nonosabasut, also loved to join in the story telling. He regaled them with stories of great caribou hunts long ago when he was a boy. He told them of the fierce northern people who lived in the frozen land. He described the land of ice, the home of the great white bears that his father and grandfather had seen.

He told the children stories his father and grandfather had told him. Stories he had been told of ships with tall sails coming to the island and taking their people away, many, many years ago. He told them how those people never returned.

Often he would begin his storytelling with, "Many years ago when my grandfather was a boy." That was the signal for Ojjbawitt to crawl up onto his lap and Mandolee to sit at his knee, to hear the next chapter of his long and exciting story.

Shanadee had noticed that lately Shanawdithit had begun to make drawings on birch bark with the charred end of sticks from burned out fires. She would sit, while the adults told the stories, and draw her pictures. Sometimes she used odemet to color the people red. Shanadee was amazed how well her daughter's drawings captured the stories.

She punched little holes in her daughter's drawings, strung them on a piece of fishing line, and proudly displayed them along the wall of their wigwam. Every time someone came by she would show them off.

Tonight was Nonosabasut's turn to tell a story, and the children had settled into their usual positions as he began in his deep voice.

"Many years ago when my grandfather was a boy, he lived up north in the land of ice. He lived with his brother, his mother, and his father. The winters were very long, and very, very cold. To keep from freezing, they had to wear heavy fur coats with large hoods to cover their heads and heavy mittens to cover their hands."

Shanadee smiled happily, as she watched the anticipation in her children's upturned faces. This was a new story, one they had not heard before. Even Shanawdithit was intently watching her uncle's scarred face, waiting for his words to form pictures in her mind. In her hand she held a charcoal stick, and on her lap was a large piece of birch bark.

"The people who lived in the land of ice were called S'kiemoos. They were shorter people than us. They kept many dogs to pull their sleds."

"What did their dogs look like?" asked Shanawdithit.

"They looked like the moisamadrook. They were very strong and very beautiful, but also sometimes very fierce."

Shanawdithit began to draw.

"My grandfather and his family lived on the edge of one of the S'kiemoos villages. It was near the sea. The villagers were friendly people and they taught our family how to build snow houses like the ones they lived in. They cut large blocks of snow and stacked them on top of each other in a big circle. As the walls went up, each block leaned a little toward the center until they eventually met at the top to form the roof. All the cracks and seams were stuffed with snow so that no wind could get through. They added a tiny round doorway to crawl through to get inside."

"How big were they, uncle Nono.?"

"They were big like our mamateeks, not big like our wigwams. They were barely high enough to stand up in," he replied, spreading his arms wide to show them. "They were only big enough for one family."

"Great white bears live in that land," Nonosabasut continued in a hushed voice. He had the complete attention of everyone around the fire. The children were hanging on to every word. Shanawdithit had looked up from her drawing and was intently watching him.

"Those bears are much bigger than our black bear; probably twice as big. Because they are white, they are very hard to see in the snow. One day a great white bear entered the village. It killed one of the S'kiemoos and two of his sled dogs. The villagers were very angry, and they were afraid for their children. They decided to hunt the great bear. My grandfather's father decided to join the hunt with the villagers."

"Did you ever see the white bear, uncle Nono?" asked Mandolee, in a voice filled with wonder.

"Yes Mandolee, I have. I saw one before I came to the Great Lake, when I lived on the coast. It came from the sea on the ice pans. It was a very big bear."

"Were you scared, uncle Nono?"

"No, Mandolee. This bear did not harm anyone. Not like the one at my great grandfather's village."

"What did the villagers do?" asked Shanawdithit, wanting him to get back to the story.

"The villagers tracked the bear with their dogs. They found him in a snow cave, near the frozen sea. The dogs drew him out of the cave. The villagers had him surrounded. There was a fierce battle. The bear was very strong. The villagers stabbed the mighty bear with many spears. My great grandfather was hit by the sharp claws of the bear. His face was scarred like mine."

Little Ojjbawitt reached up his hand and ran his chubby fingers over the deep scar in Nonosabasut's chin. "Was it like this, uncle?"

"No, little one," he said affectionately. Taking his nephew's tiny hand in his, he reached up to his hairline and traced a line down his cheek and across his nose to the other side of his face. "That's where the bear marked him."

Every spring the main camp was broken up and most of the tribe would leave the Great Lake to move down river in smaller groups. Shanadee had avoided this for years. She did not want to have an encounter with the Buggishaman. Now that she had children she was even more reluctant to leave the Great Lake and risk exposing them to the dangers she knew were out there. Although Kirradittii made the trip to the coast most years, it had been almost 20 years since Shanadee had been there.

Over the past few years there had been very few reports of trouble with the Buggishaman. The tribe had learned to become invisible and avoided contact as much as possible. It seemed to be working; at least that was what Kirradittii kept telling her.

Through his persistent coaxing, he had convinced her to move down river for the summer to be closer to the coast and have better access to the plentiful food supply it offered. She had reluctantly agreed and they left with their family in early May. They followed the river for three days until Shanadee decided they were close enough. There they built a mamateek in a small clearing near the river. Tall birch trees circled the clearing and a little trickling brook wound its way around the edge, eventually finding its way into the larger river. Shanadee thought it was a perfect place for their summer camp.

After a week, three other families joined them and built mamateeks in the clearing as well. Shanadee felt even better then. She always felt safer with more people around. Nevertheless, both Shanadee and Kirradittii repeatedly told their children to run into the woods and hide at the first sign of the Buggishaman.

The summer had gone by quickly, and they had been able to collect plenty of food from the coast without incident. It was

September. The days were getting shorter and the air was getting colder. It was time to prepare to return to the winter camp at the Great Lake before the first snows came. There they would once again reunite with the other families of the tribe to spend the winter. The larger group always made Shanadee feel safer.

Through the summer Shanadee had grown a little more comfortable at the summer camp. She had even gone to the coast with Kirradittii and Jaywritt on one occasion. Still she knew she would never be worry free until they were back at the Great Lake.

"Let's do one last hunt in the morning," Shanadee whispered in Kirradittii's ear, as they lay side by side in their mamateek. "Just you and me, like old times," she murmured softly, so as not to wake the sleeping children.

"Why not," he replied sleepily. "Shanawdithit can watch her brother and sister. Besides, I still need one more chance to beat you at shooting."

"Never happen," she laughed, and poked him playfully in the side.

Kirradittii wrapped his arm around her and pulled her close as he drifted back to sleep. Life is good, he thought, as he listened to the comforting sounds of his sleeping family.

At the campfire last night, the conversation had quickly turned from the usual stories of their ancestors to the trip back up river to the Great Lake. The summer was being pushed out by the cool fall winds, and all around the forest was painted in shades of orange and gold. Soon the trees would shake off their leaves and before long the first snow would blanket their bare spindly branches. As happened at this time every year, the change in seasons served to draw the tribe back to the winter camp with its promise of safety and peace. Two of the four families had decided they would be leaving early and they had everything prepared to begin the trip back up river in the morning. Before the evening was over, Jaywritt had announced he would also be leaving with them in the morning.

"Get up children. Your uncle is leaving today," said Shanadee.

Ojjbawitt scurried out of bed and toddled out the door in search of his uncle. The two girls took a little longer, but soon they were all standing outside the mamateek where Jaywritt was kneeling on the ground lashing the last of his things to the rack he would carry on his shoulders.

When he finished, he held out his arms and Ojjbawitt ran into them. "Don't go and leave us uncle Jaywritt," he sobbed.

"I will see you in a few days, little fella," he said hugging him tightly. "Come here girls," he said releasing one arm from Ojjbawitt and holding it out to them.

Shanadee watched him fondly. It took her back to when he was just a toddler like Ojjbawitt. She noticed the moisture in his eyes as he looked over the girls' heads and met her eyes. He smiled sheepishly and began to untangle himself from the group hug. Ojjbawitt was the last to let go. With his chubby little arms wrapped tightly around Jaywritt's neck, he was determined to keep his uncle from leaving.

Jaywritt gently pulled him loose, kissed him on the cheek and handed him to his mother. "Take good care of them," he said. "I will see you at the Lake."

Jaywritt turned and followed the others along the river path. Before he disappeared into the trees, he turned and gave a final wave to the three children standing in the clearing. "Bye uncle Jaywritt," they chorused.

Shanadee felt a little anxious leaving the children at the camp with such a small number of people. It had seemed safer when there were more families camped there. She knew there were no settlers in the area and they had not had any encounters during the summer. They would not be going far to hunt, so it should be safe, she reasoned. Still she wished Jaywritt had stayed another day

She listened as Kirradittii gave Shanawdithit her instructions.

"Now Shanawdithit, you keep a sharp watch. Take your brother and sister into the woods at the first sign of danger," he instructed her. "No matter what happens, you run. While we are gone, stay near the camp where it is safe," he said. "Don't let your brother or your sister wander off anywhere. You are the oldest, and I'm counting on you."

"I will, Father. Don't worry, we'll be safe. I will watch over them."

"Stop fussing Kirradittii," said Shanadee, inwardly pleased that he had the same anxiety as she did. "Shanawdithit will look after them. Let's go."

Kirradittii and Shanadee picked up their hathemays, one long and one short, settled them on their shoulders and headed across the clearing towards the woods. Just before entering the trees, Kirradittii turned for one last look and waved to the three children standing outside the mamateek door.

"See you soon," he yelled.

"See you father," they chorused.

This time Kirradittii took the lead. He loved these times alone with Shanadee. Since the children had arrived they hadn't done much of this. There never seemed to be any time. Maybe that will change now that Shanawdithit is getting older, he thought, as he walked along.

Although the sun was overhead in the sky, a light rain began to fall. It seemed to refresh the land and served to lift his spirits. This was going to be a good day. He had a good feeling about it. He turned and glanced over his shoulder at Shanadee. She was smiling at him as if she had read his mind. Sometimes he suspected she really could do that.

The light drizzle passed as quickly as it had arrived, leaving the trees wet and glistening in the sunlight. Tiny drops of water trickled down the orange and red leaves, stretched as if clinging to safety before finally falling to the ground below. The sunlight sparkled and shimmered through the falling drops, creating around them a shiny twinkling world of changing color. Shanadee held out her hand to catch some of the tumbling drops, laughing with delight.

Kirradittii had stopped on the path and was watching her girlish reaction with amusement. She never stopped surprising him. He loved times like this when the layers were peeled back from the tough exterior she always displayed in public; when he got to see the real girl that hid beneath. Standing there, with her face turned upward and hands outstretched towards the dancing droplets, she looked younger and more beautiful than the first time he had seen her. Right now he thought he was the luckiest man alive.

"Look," she said breaking the spell

He turned and looked over his shoulder where she was pointing. Through the trees he could see the shimmering, mirror surface of a small pond. Not a ripple stirred the water. It was as if the light rain had never been there. He thought it must be the source of the trickling brook they had been following.

Silently they crept through the protective tangle of brush to the water's edge where they could see the whole pond. From this spot they could see from one end all the way down to the other.

"It's empty," whispered Kirradittii.

"Ducks or Geese will come. Let's just wait for a while," she replied softly.

"Maybe. Let's hide there in those thick bushes."

They crawled under the low hanging bushes and waited. Sitting on the ground, shoulder to shoulder, they shared unspoken companionship. The hunter's need to be quiet did not encroach on their close contact, nor did the enforced silence grow awkward or strained. They had been together long enough to understand that talking was not the only way to communicate. They were comfortable in shared silence. And so they sat there simply enjoying each other's company.

It wasn't very long before they heard the approaching honk of the first flock of geese approaching over the trees. Kirradittii cupped his hands around his mouth, and called them. Shanadee was always amazed at the way he could perfectly mimic them. They came from the north, soaring low over the trees at the far end of the pond, and settled in the water closer to the center.

Together they released their first arrows, both finding their mark. Kirradittii wasn't as fast as his wife in getting a second arrow in flight, and his fell harmlessly into the water as the large birds spread their huge wings and took flight, leaving three of their flock flailing and splashing on the surface below them.

Smiling broadly, he punched Shanadee playfully on the arm. "You did it again! You beat your husband."

"No match," she replied mischievously. "I'll go and get the birds," she said, as she dropped her hathemay and slipped out of her clothes. Although they had never talked about it, she had known for some time that Kirradittii had a deadly fear of water, and that he had never learned to swim.

Kirradittii looked on with admiration as she waded out into the chilly water, and dove smoothly underneath the surface. He knew she had discovered his fear of water and was avoiding bringing it up because she did not want him to feel embarrassed. She was a good wife that way, he thought, as he watched her body glide effortlessly through the quiet water. He was so glad he had found her.

He watched as Shanadee snagged the three birds and snapped each of their necks to make sure they were dead. Holding the three arrows, she towed the birds back to shore where Kirradittii was sitting on the ground.

Wading out of the pond she stood directly in front of him and held out the birds, "I went out there and got them, so now you can carry them," she said tauntingly.

"I can do that," he said, staring admiringly at her, watching the dripping water meander its way down over her bare skin. "You just made it worthwhile," he whispered hoarsely, as he reached for her and pulled her down on him.

Shanadee smiled down at him, as she picked up her cloak and slipped it over her head. "We should get back to camp. I don't like the children there alone."

The mention of the children served to break the spell for Kirradittii and he reluctantly gathered up his hathemay and the three geese. "Alright then, let's go," he said, as he slung the three birds over his shoulder. He reached out to Shanadee, pulled her against him, gave her a lingering kiss, turned and broke into a trot in the direction of the camp.

Shanadee stood there for a moment, grinning after him while shaking her head in amusement. "You make me very happy, Kirradittii," she called after him and followed him down the trail.

Ahead of her he raised his closed fist in the air in acknowledgement.

A short while later, they walked into the clearing and they both breathed a sigh of relief at seeing the children were alright. Shanawdithit was sitting on the grassy river bank, keeping an eye on her brother and sister who were playing in the shallow water. Her head was bent over a square of birch bark that she held on her lap. She appeared to be drawing her brother and sister at play.

Now that two of the families had left, there was only one other mamateek occupied beside Kirradittii's. It was on the other side of the clearing close to the river bank. Doodlebewshet and her mother were sitting in front of the door working on baskets for the trip back up river. Her father was gathering firewood at the edge of the clearing.

To Kirradittii, the scene that was spread before him looked perfect.

"Everything well?" he asked as he walked pass the two women.

"Everything is fine Kirradittii. There is no one around but us," replied Doodlebewshet. "It's been a really quiet day."

"Look what we have," Kirradittii shouted, as he approached the river bank. Tossing the birds down on the beach, he said, "Here son, help your sisters clean them for supper."

In his haste to reach the birds, Ojjbawitt tripped and fell on his face in the water, and had to be rescued by Mandolee. He was pulled to his feet spitting and sputtering, but still struggling to get to the birds first.

"Let me go, Mandolee. Let me go!" he yelled, pulling his arm free and sloshing through the water to reach the geese.

Shanawdithit put aside the drawing, anchored it to the ground with a small stone, and joined her brother and sister at the water's edge. She selected one of the remaining two birds and gave the other to Mandolee. Ojjbawitt had picked the biggest goose and had his arms wrapped around it possessively.

"Sure you can handle that one son?" laughed Kirradittii.

"Yes father," said Ojjbawitt, grinning proudly.

Kirradittii knew he was too young to clean the bird and Shanawdithit would have to finish it for him, but it was fun watching him try.

Kirradittii lingered for a few minutes, and watched Shanawdithit show them how to pull the feathers from the dead birds. All three were busy plucking the geese when he turned and walked back to the nearest mamateek. Shanadee was inside with a pot of water positioned over the fire. She was preparing to boil one of the geese for the evening meal. Kirradittii crept up behind her, wrapped his arms around her and squeezed her playfully.

Down on the beach, Shanawdithit was bent over one of the geese, pulling out its insides, when the water around her was sprayed like a shower from a sudden rainstorm. She felt something bite into her hand, and then she heard the gunshot. Instinctively she grabbed her brother and scrambled up the riverbank, pushing Mandolee ahead of her. Her hand felt as though it was burning, and a thin line of blood trickled down her upraised arm. As she cleared the top of the bank on her hands and knees, she saw her father and mother racing across the clearing. Her mother had her hathemay in one hand and a sheath of arrows in the other. Shanawdithit grabbed her sister's hand and ran toward them. Kirradittii took Ojjbawitt from her and herded them in the direction of the woods behind their mamateek.

"Keep running and hide in the woods!" her mother shouted to them as she continued racing in the direction of the river.

Over on the left, Shanawdithit saw Doodlebewshet hustling her mother into the woods behind their mamateek. Doodlebewshet's father ran out of the door of their mamateek with his hathemay in his hand. He was running toward the river too.

Just as Shanawdithit reached the edge of the clearing she heard more gunshots. Anxiously she turned and looked back towards the river bank. Out in the middle of the river she saw a small boat with two of the dreaded Buggishaman. One was moving the boat with long sticks he pulled through the water, the other was standing in the front pointing a long stick in their direction that spat fire. *A gun,* she suddenly realized with fear.

She watched her mother launch several arrows at the approaching boat, then she turned and ran after her father.

After each shot, Shanadee ran a few steps to confuse the Buggishaman's gun that was now concentrating on her. She knew if the Buggishaman continued to fire at her Kirradittii could get the children safely into the woods.

With satisfaction, Shanadee saw her arrows were falling into the boat amongst the two Buggishaman. Out on her right she saw that Doodlebewshet's father had joined her and was firing arrows at the boat as well.

"Keep moving. Don't stand in one place," she yelled as another shot tore into the side of the mamateek behind her. Instinctively she ducked and ran a little to her left, releasing two more arrows as she stopped. She saw the Buggishaman fall against the side of the boat and the gun tumble into the water. She wasn't sure if he had been thrown off balance by the rocking boat or had been hit by one of their arrows. Either way, the gun had gone into the water and that left him unarmed.

The old hatred that had been lurking below the surface returned in a rush. They had tried to kill her children. They needed to die for that! "Keep firing," she yelled. "He can't shoot at us anymore. We must kill them! Hurry, before they get away."

The fallen Buggishaman pulled himself up from the bottom of the boat and grabbed one of the sticks. Hurriedly, they pushed the boat back out into the current, letting it take them back downstream. They had not been prepared for this kind of reception, nor had they expected the Beothuk to be so accurate with their arrows. They had always heard the Red Indians ran away from the White Man. These two weren't running, they were actually fighting back.

Screaming some high pitched war cry that just seemed to spill out of her, Shanadee raced along the riverbank and let fly two more volleys before the boat was carried out of range. She thought she had hit one of the White Devils. The rushing current carried them around the bend and out of sight. She could still hear them shouting in that strange language as they floated down the river.

Shanadee stood there on the riverbank waiting for her pounding heart to return to normal. She listened until the shouting faded in the distance, then she turned and jogged back to camp and followed Kirradittii's trail into the woods. She found her family sitting next to a brook. Kirradittii was washing and dressing the wound on Shanawdithit's hand. Kirradittii looked at her with relief as she hugged Ojjbawitt and Mandolee.

"What happened back there?"

"They got away."

"Did you hit either one?"

"I think I did, but I'm not sure. Anyway, they are gone now. What happened to Shanawdithit?"

"She was hit in the hand."

"Let me see."

Shanadee gently took her daughter's arm and turned it over. The shot had passed completely through her hand. It seemed it hadn't broken any bones in its passing.

"You were lucky," she said, as she wiped the tears from Shanawdithit face. "This will heal and you will only have a small scar to show for it. One like I have on my arm. It will always remind you how evil the Buggishaman is."

"Are they hurt?" she asked Kirradittii nodding in the direction of the other two children.

"Neither Ojjbawitt nor Mandolee were hit by the shooting. Shanawdithit got them away safely. She saved their lives today."

"You did well, Shanawdithit," said Shanadee. "You did really well."

"Yes," Kirradittii agreed, "you were very brave."

Both parents knew it could easily have been different. It could have been a much worse outcome. They were lucky the Buggishaman was such a poor shot.

"We are leaving now," he announced. "I am going back to camp and get a few things for the trip and we leaving for the Great Lake. We are not staying here any longer."

"I will stay here with the children," said Shanadee. "Bring Doodlebewshet and her family."

As soon as he was finished with Shanawdithit's hand, Kirradittii returned to the camp to get their belongings. This would now change their plans. They would leave tonight in case the Buggishaman decided to return under the cover of darkness. Kirradittii had no intension of waiting to find out and putting his family in any further danger.

Very little time passed before the two families were ready to travel. They only took the essentials, since they didn't want to burden themselves and slow down their flight to safety. The group of eight strung out along the path that paralleled the river.

In their hasty retreat, they had to leave most of their dried and smoked meat that was intended to get them through the winter at the Great Lake. Once his family was safe at the winter camp, Kirradittii planned to return and retrieve the supply if it was still undisturbed. For now, the only thing that concerned him was getting as far away from the Buggishaman as possible.

By the time the moon had climbed to the middle of the sky, they decided they had travelled far enough. They moved off the beaten path, and made their way inland away from the river. After a while they stopped and set up a temporary camp for the night.

While the two men were building a lean-to, the women started a small fire and roasted the three geese that Kirradittii had retrieved from the beach before they left the summer camp. There was plenty to feed the eight of them, and after they finished eating they all stretched out on the ground and fell asleep under the stars.

At least most of them slept. Kirradittii was too nervous and he lay there unable to sleep for most of the night, listening to the night sounds and thinking of what may have happened if the Buggishaman hadn't missed his mark. He could have lost his children today. He repeatedly thanked the Great Spirit for protecting his family. He was proud of his wife too, although he thought she might have been a bit reckless. Then again she did scare away the Buggishaman. That didn't happen every day.

The third day was almost spent when they reached the winter camp at the Great Lake. Kirradittii had pushed them hard to put as much distance as possible between themselves and the Buggishaman. Even though they had left many things they needed behind, all he cared about now was to get his family to safety. He had not been able to stop looking over his shoulder until he walked into the clearing and was met by Nonosabasut and Jaywritt. They were overjoyed to see their nieces and little nephew. Nonosabasut hoisted Ojjbawitt high on his bare shoulders, and paraded him around the camp.

Ojjbawitt squealed with delight. He could see everything, perched up here on his uncle's broad shoulders. Happily, he waved and yelled to the other children who crowded around Nonosabasut hoping to get a ride as well. Ojjbawitt had a firm grip on his uncle's thick braid and wasn't about to relinquish his perch anytime soon.

Shanadee and Shanawdithit carried the few belongings they had with them into Nonosabasut's wigwam. It was a good feeling to be home again. A sense of peace and safety seemed to settle over them as soon as they walked through its door.

Shanadee removed the cloth Kirradittii had wound around Shanawdithit's hand, and then she carefully checked the wound. It appeared to be healing well. Her husband had done a good job dressing it. Still, Shanawdithit would always carry the scar with her as a vivid reminder to stay away from the hated Buggishaman.

Shanadee held her daughter's hand and stared directly into her eyes. "Always remember, the Buggishaman is not to be trusted. He has killed most of our family. He will kill you if he gets a chance. Never let them see you."

"Are all Buggishaman like this, mother?"

"Some say no. I have never met one who wasn't," she replied angrily as she released her daughter's hand.

"Why do they hate us so much?"

"I don't know, Shanawdithit. All I know is that they do. I think they would kill us all if they could."

Nonosabasut pushed aside the door flap, bent almost to the ground to clear the door post and stepped inside. Ojjbawitt was still perched on his shoulders, both hands wrapped tightly around his uncle's long braid. They were followed closely by Kirradittii and Jaywritt.

"How is her hand?" asked Kirradittii.

"It is fine. You did well, my husband."

Kirradittii smiled at Shanadee in appreciation.

Nonosabasut lowered Ojjbawitt to the ground and sat next to the fire. Ojjbawitt immediately climbed up onto his uncle's lap. Looking up into his twinkling eyes he said, "Tell a story."

Nonosabasut chuckled and began. "Many, many, years ago when my grandfather was the age of Shanawdithit, he came to live on this beautiful island. Before that he lived in the frozen land with his mother and father. They lived in a village with the S'kiemoos. The villagers sometimes crossed the water to the island to hunt for food. When they returned to the frozen land, they told stories of a red people like my grandfather's family."

"Was that us, uncle Nono?" asked Mandolee.

"Not us. We were not even born then. It was our ancestors though."

"What's an ancestor?" asked Ojjbawitt.

"Well my little one, ancestors are our families who lived long before us and are now in the land of Gossett. It's like your grandparents and their grandparents before them. They are all our ancestors."

"So what did your grandfather do, uncle Nono?" asked Mandolee eagerly.

"When he heard the stories it made him long to see more Red Indians. He begged his parents to let him travel to the island with the villagers. At first they would not agree. They were afraid he would not return and they would never see him again."

"Why did they think that?"

"Because those trips were very dangerous, and sometimes not all of the travelers returned."

"Oh my!" said Mandolee.

"Finally, after much begging he convinced his parents to let him take the trip."

"They must have been really scared for him though."

"I'm sure they were, but he set out on the trip in the month of May with a small group of men. It was the time when the great ice pans began to move along the coast. They pushed their wooden boat over the surface of the ice pans. Where there was open water they used the boat to reach the next ice island. It was a lot of hard work and very dangerous too. Sometimes they would ride the ice pans and let the ocean current take them toward the island."

"How big were the pans?"

"They were very, very, big. Some were as large as a lake. Some were big enough to build a whole village on."

"On the second day they could see land far in the distance. It was so far away it was just blue shapes at the end of the sky. They launched the boat back into the ocean, and followed channels of open water around the giant ice pans until they were closer to the land. A larger pan lay between them and the shoreline. They decided it would be easier to cross it than to go all the way around, so they pulled the boat up onto the ice."

"They were getting near the other side of the ice pan when a sharp crack sounded and with a loud groan the ice broke into pieces underneath their feet. The boat, and all but two men, fell into the opening. My grandfather was one of the two."

"What about the others, Uncle?"

"They were all crushed by the ice, as the sea lifted the two pieces back together. The piece of the ice pan my grandfather and his friend were on floated along the coast for two more days. They were very cold and hungry. They had lost everything with the boat. On the third day, they were close enough to land to see a group of Indians on the shore. My grandfather yelled and waved to them. Hearing their own language, the Indians launched their tapaithook and rescued them from the ice. Then they took them back to their camp."

"Did he ever see his parents again," asked Shanawdithit. Tonight she sat and watched her uncle. She could not draw because of her bandaged hand.

"He never returned to the frozen land again."

"That's sad," she whispered.

Part Two

The year 1811 has often been considered to be the pivotal point for the ill-fated Beothuk nation. It was in January of that year that Shanadee and her family determined the events that they believed would ensure their survival. History, however, would write a much different story.

Chapter 12
1811
BUCHAN

Once again the leaves were turning to red and gold. Soon the winds would come and the trees would shake off these bright colors and retreat within themselves to await the warm winds of spring. This change also brought the tribe home to the winter camp at the Great Lake. As each band arrived they brought with them the supplies of food gathered throughout the summer. Nonosabasut had supervised the distribution of these supplies to the three storehouses built around the lake. From what he saw it had been a good summer and plenty of food had been stored up to get them through the long, unpredictable winter. Nonosabasut was happy with what they had stored. There should be no fear of anyone going hungry this year.

Over the years, three separate camps had been set up around the Great Lake. The main camp, where Nonosabasut lived, was built close to the end of the lake, near the source of the Great River. A second camp was across on the other side of the Lake, and the third was on the same side as the main camp, but on the far end of the Lake. Nonosabasut had made sure each camp had its own storehouse and that they were all in good condition. The food had been distributed to these storehouses based on the number of people in each camp. While the storehouses were being filled, Nonosabasut had visited the other two camps and counted the tribe members. He had counted thirty at those sites and forty-two at the main camp. That was a total of seventy-two people. There had been ninety-eight two years ago when he had done his last count. Each year the tribe was getting smaller. He worried about the future of his people. Sometimes he wondered if there could be a future. Maybe the numbers were already too small for a recovery. It was troubling.

The snow had fallen for many days. There wasn't much to do but stay inside. Each morning when Nonosabasut opened his eyes, he wondered if this was going to be another day of doing nothing like yesterday and the day before.

This morning something was different. At first he wasn't sure what it was, he just sensed that something had changed.

Pushing himself up on his elbow and shaking his head to clear the fog of sleep, he realized something had awakened him. There was very little daylight filtering through the smoke hole in the roof, so it was earlier than he would normally wake. Everyone else in the wigwam seemed to be asleep. So what was it that had awakened him?

There! There it was again! It sounded like someone talking, barely above a whisper, just outside the wigwam. Then he detected a shuffling through the snow. What were people doing out there so early in the morning, wondered Nonosabasut?

Suddenly the chilly fingers of fear slid along his spine. He understood what he was hearing through the thin walls. The dreaded Buggishaman! They were here, right outside the wigwam!

Quietly pushing back the thick covering of animal skins, he crawled out of his bed and crept through the dim light to his brother and Shanadee sleeping next to the children. Gently shaking his brother awake, he whispered in his ear, "We have big trouble. The Buggishaman is here."

Overhearing his whisper, Shanadee threw off the covers and frantically scrambled to her feet. She grabbed the nearest hathemay from the rack.

Holding up his hand, Nonosabasut urgently whispered, "No. Don't make them shoot. Let me see how many are out there. Wake the children, but keep them quiet. They must be ready to run."

Inwardly nervous but outwardly calm, Nonosabasut walked to the door, pushed the flap aside and, empty handed, stepped outside into the early dawn to face their most dangerous enemy.

Standing around the clearing he saw many Buggishaman. They all had guns. They were circled around each of the three wigwams. There would be no escape this time.

Over his shoulder he said, "Keep the children inside Shanadee. There are too many of them."

Behind him, he was aware of Shanadee and Kirradittii stepping through the door. They were closely followed by Jaywritt. Shanadee and Kirradittii came to stand on either side of him. Both of them had their hathemays in their hands, with arrows already notched.

"Stay inside by the door," Shanadee hissed to the three children behind her. "If they shoot their guns, run into the woods and don't look back. Just keep running no matter what. Do you hear me, Shanawdithit?"

"Yes mother," came the trembling reply from inside the wigwam. She thought she heard a soft sob from Mandolee.

Nonosabasut looked around the clearing at the many guns that were leveled at them and his heart felt very heavy. This was the day they would die. He should have heard them coming. He should not have grown careless. He was their leader. How could he have let this happen? He should have done better.

Fear had a firm grip on him. It had slipped its icy fingers around his chest and was squeezing. He had to work at breathing. Even though it was cold enough to see your breath, he could feel the sweat on his arms and trickling down his back inside his thick cloak. What are they doing so far from the coast, he wondered? Why haven't they shot their guns yet? What are they up to?

Many of the tribe members had come out of the wigwams, and were standing silently in the softly falling snow. They were looking toward Nonosabasut, anxiously waiting for him to tell them what to do. Nonosabasut saw his fear reflected in their eyes and in the way the mothers held their children close to them. He noticed how the fathers had pushed their families behind them in an effort to shield them. He realized how hopeless this was and his stomach rolled.

The air was thick with tension.

The silence was unnerving.

Both enemies stared at each other, separated by years of mistrust and violence.

He wondered what would trigger the shooting. He wondered if there was any way he could stop it.

He knew he had to try.

"Do not raise your hathemays," he said quietly to Kirradittii and Shanadee. "Stay calm, Shanadee," he whispered. He knew that right now she would be wrestling with her fierce hatred of the Buggishaman. Like him, she was probably overwhelmed with the hopelessness of their situation. She might even now be calculating how many she could bring down before they got her. He needed her to be under control. The smallest sign of aggression was bound to get them all killed.

"Don't provoke them," he shouted to the tribe, knowing the Buggishaman did not understand his language any more then he understood theirs. "Don't do anything to make them nervous. If they start shooting it's all over for us. Just wait to see what they do. Try to stay calm."

As he was talking, Nonosabasut noticed one of the men, who had been in quiet conversation with two other Buggishaman, stop and turn in his direction. He was a tall man, almost as tall as me thought Nonosabasut. He wore a very short black beard that made his face even longer. He was thin, very thin; a man in need of a good meal. The heavy, fur lined, leather coat hung loose on him. Maybe one time he had filled it out, certainly not anymore.

Nonosabasut thought he might be their leader. He had noticed the other Buggishaman seemed to be taking direction from him.

He lifted his hand in Nonosabasut's direction and said something. His men glanced around nervously at each other and slowly lowered their guns until they were pointing at the snow. They did not, however, take their eyes off Shanadee, Kirradittii and several others who were holding their bows in their hands. Each side eyed the other suspiciously. The moment hung on a thin wire of mistrust.

In the unnatural silence Nonosabasut was sure he could hear his own heart beating, and it was beating a lot faster than usual.

The tall Buggishaman gestured to Nonosabasut, and then to the other Buggishaman, pulled off his gloves and held both his empty hands up for him to see.

Slowly he approached Nonosabasut. His boots stirred up little flurries of the soft, fluffy snow that blanketed the clearing. Nothing else moved.

He continued to hold his empty hands out in front of him as he walked toward Nonosabasut. He stopped about two hathemay lengths away.

Nonosabasut felt Shanadee tense at his side. A quick sideways glance confirmed what he had expected. Her knuckles were white from the severe grip she had on the hathemay. Her face was an angry mask, unmoving, as if carved from stone.

"Don't!" he warned her, as he turned back to face the Buggishaman.

"Kirradittii," he said sternly, desperately hoping his brother could control his wife.

"Be patient," he heard Kirradittii whisper to Shanadee. "Don't put the children at risk."

"What do you think they want?" asked Nonosabasut.

"To kill us," hissed Shanadee.

"Why haven't they done it yet? They could have if they wanted to."

"It's a trick," said Shanadee from behind. She had stepped back next to Jaywritt. They were standing protectively in front of the wigwam door.

"Do you think we should run for it and take our chances?" asked Kirradittii, nervously.

"No!" muttered Nonosabasut. "See how he shows us his hands are empty. I think he is trying to tell us he does not mean to hurt us. If we run the shooting will start."

"Maybe you are right," said Kirradittii.

"How many do you see?"

"I count 18," said Shanadee.

"There are too many. They all have guns. We would not have a chance against them. Let's wait," said Nonosabasut.

"Bouthland," called the thin man over his shoulder, "bring me those presents."

"Yes sir, Lieut'nt Buchan," replied one of the men as he turned and started to run toward the edge of the clearing.

Shanadee raised her hathemay to the firing position.

"No running man!" shouted Buchan. "You want to get yourself killed? Don't go making any sudden movements. That goes for all of you."

Bouthland glanced nervously at the Indians with the bows, and continued across the clearing at a much slower pace. He selected one of the heavily laden sleds and, with the help of one other man, pulled it across the clearing to where Buchan was waiting.

Nonosabasut watched them uneasily. What was under the cover on that sled? It couldn't be more guns. They had plenty of them already. He knew if he made a wrong move here everyone at the camp could be killed. He felt every eye in the tribe on him, waiting for some sign as they shuffled nervously in the bitter cold, blankets drawn tightly around them. Their breath hung suspended in a frozen cloud, drifting slowly over their heads.

These people were his responsibility. He had to do the right thing. He had no reason to trust the Buggishaman, yet they were acting friendly. He glanced at his brother for some sign.

He got none.

Kirradittii, like all the others, was counting on him to make the decision.

He decided to wait to see what this Buggishaman would do. What choice did he have anyway?

Buchan dropped to one knee in the snow next to the sled. With a knife he cut the frozen rope that secured the bundle to the sled, and then fished two colored blankets from one of the bags. Pushing to his feet, he dropped the knife on the sled and stepped closer to Nonosabasut holding the blankets out in front of him.

Seeing there were only blankets in the bag, Nonosabasut found himself relaxing just a little. He stepped forward, closing the gap between them. He stood there for a long time, looking directly into the Buggishaman's eyes. He could find no anger there.

Maybe this will be alright, he thought. He held out his hand and accepted the gift from the Buggishaman. He turned and handed one of the blankets to Kirradittii.

Buchan smiled broadly and nodded. Patting his chest repeatedly he said "Buchan." Pointing at Nonosabasut he asked, "What is your name?"

Understanding his intention, Nonosabasut replied, "Nonosabasut," and patted his chest like the Buggishaman had.

Nonosabasut pointed and said "Bukn." Around the group of Red Indians the awkward word was repeated, as though they were sampling its taste in their mouths for the first time.

Buchan smiled and nodded. Behind him Bouthland murmured, "I think they got you, Lieut'nt, sir."

Buchan then motioned toward the sled carrying the blankets, and swung his hands around the clearing.

"I think he wants to give everyone blankets," Kirradittii said to Nonosabasut.

"I think so brother, but we must be careful." Over Kirradittii's shoulder, he saw Shanadee glowering at the thin man, hatred simmering in her dark eyes.

Their eyes met, and Nonosabasut shook his head from side to side. He knew she had every right to hate them, but now was not a good time to act on it.

Turning back to Buchan, he nodded his consent, gesturing at the groups in front of each wigwam.

Two of Buchan's men began moving around the clearing, handing out the blankets to the tribe members. Many of them shook them out and wrapped them around their shoulders to shield against the cold wind.

The explosive tension had eased, at least for the moment.

Nonosabasut said loudly to the crowd gathered behind him, "Prepare food for them. We will have a meal with these Buggishaman."

With that, several of the women moved out of the crowd and went into the largest wigwam.

Nonosabasut turned back to face Buchan. "Do you intend to kill us?" He asked the Buggishaman.

"He has no idea what you said," Kirradittii whispered.

"Then you have no need to whisper, my brother," smiled Nonosabasut.

He looked directly at Buchan again, studying his eyes. It was just as before, there was no anger to be seen in this man's eyes.

Pointing his finger at him, he lifted a stick as if it were a gun, and pretended to shoot several of the tribe standing nearby. "Bang, bang," he said.

The Buggishaman seemed to understand, raised his hands to chest level, palms facing Nonosabasut, and shook his head, no.

Buchan turned and ordered his men to lay their guns on the snow covered ground. Some of the men hesitated and looked at each other for reassurance before following the order, but within a few moments they had all emptied their hands. Buchan then looked expectantly at Kirradittii and Shanadee's bows.

"He wants you to put down your hathemay," Nonosabasut said to his brother and his wife. "He has shown us a sign of peace. We must do the same."

Hesitantly, Kirradittii walked to the wigwam and propped his hathemay against its side. He slid the sheath of arrows from his shoulder, and placed it next to the hathemay. Shanadee stood rigidly, unmoving. Kirradittii touched her on the arm and whispered in her ear. Angrily, she swirled around and disappeared through the door of their wigwam.

All around the clearing the other armed Beothuks laid aside their weapons as well.

Nonosabasut folded his blanket, dropped it on the ground and sat on it. Buchan did the same.

So began a drawn out conversation in pantomime between the two leaders that carried on until they were interrupted by those preparing the food.

Nonosabasut found that drawing pictures in the snow, as he had seen Shanawdithit do on birch bark, helped him and Buchan understand each other. He found Buchan was a very curious man. He wanted to see everything the tribe used in everyday life. Nonosabasut had people bring everything from drinking and cooking containers, to the hathemay and even odemet. Bukn examined each with much care and asked many questions. Sometimes he made drawings like Nonosabasut had seen Shanawdithit make. Nonosabasut demonstrated the making and use of each item. The more he talked to this man the more comfortable he felt.

Buchan pointed to a snow covered tapaithook. Nonosabasut nodded and they pushed themselves to their feet. Followed by a large group of Buggishaman and Beothuk, they walked to the mound of snow. Nonosabasut and Kirradittii brushed the snow away and then righted the overturned tapaithook. Buchan seemed to be very interested in this one. He looked at it from the end, from the sides, from the top and the bottom. He was still examining it when they were told the food was ready.

Holding out his hand, Nonosabasut indicated they should go into the wigwam. Kirradittii walked ahead and held the flap open for them to enter.

"Do you think we should all go in there?" asked Corporal Butler, anxiously. "That would be an easy trap. There might even be something in the food."

"We will take some of our food and share with them as well," replied Buchan. "You pick three men and stay outside just in case. Bring me the second sled with the rest of the presents", he continued.

"Yes sir. Probably just as well. Don't expect their food would sit well with me anyway."

Butler, and two of the other marines, walked back to the edge of the ice where they had left the sleds. They returned, pulling the heavy laden sleds behind them. Unloading food from one and presents from the other they carried the supplies inside the large wigwam and deposited them in a pile against one of the walls. Butler then selected three of the men and returned outside to stand watch.

Buchan selected dried jerky from one of the bags and handed it around the closest group of Beothuk. They all stood watching their chief, unwilling to take the first bite. Buchan then took a bite of the piece he was holding in his hand and chewed vigorously, nodding encouragement to Nonosabasut.

Looking around him at the tribe members standing there with the jerky held in their hands, Nonosabasut tentatively took a bite, and grinned with delight at the salty taste. Around the large tent murmurs of appreciation arose as the whole tribe sampled the dried meat together.

Turning to Buchan, Nonosabasut indicated a spot near the fire and then took a seat on the ground. Buchan sat next to him and, as though they had all been waiting for this confirmation, everyone found a place on the ground. Only those serving the food remained standing.

Two large iron pots, which had been taken from settlers, were hanging over the fire. The women dipped a thick liquid broth from the steaming pots with small birch bark containers. The mouth-watering smell of the meat stew drifted around the crowded room, drawing everyone's attention to its source. For a few moments it served its intended purpose in establishing a common bond between Red Indian and Buggishaman.

Several of the women moved among the crowd and passed around the containers of stew. One of Buchan's men handed out several loaves of bread and each person tore a piece from the loaf as it passed by. Taking the lead, Buchan dipped his in the steaming broth, stuffed the dripping bread into his mouth and chewed with obvious relish. Nonosabasut followed his example, and soon the wigwam was abuzz with the contented sounds of grown men enjoying a hot meal to the exclusion of all else.

The meal was a drawn out affair that lasted until the middle of the day, but that was not all that unusual. Nonosabasut had enjoyed many feasts just as long. The unusual thing was that this one was with Buggishaman. This was something different, something he had never done before. He had spent most of the meal in animated pantomime with Buchan. Although he couldn't talk in the strange language, he had a pretty good idea what the man was saying.

Nonosabasut gathered from Buchan that he had stored more gifts at a camp several hours down river, and it was his intention to go and get them and bring them back for the tribe. Bukn seemed to want him to go with him to pick up the gifts. Although Nonosabasut was enjoying the company of this Bukn, he was still a little uneasy. This was all happening so fast!

"What do you think of all this?" he asked Kirradittii.

Shanadee, who was standing near her husband, responded before Kirradittii could.

"Don't go Nonosabasut. They will kill you. He knows you are the chief. He just wants to draw you away from here because you are our leader."

Kirradittii was torn. He had learned to trust his wife's instincts, but there was something about this Buggishaman that seemed right. Maybe there was a chance that things could get better between the two nations. He could tell his brother was waging a fierce internal battle. A half day of bonding with Bukn could never erase the damage that had been done to their people over the past years. But none of them had the power to change the past. Maybe they could change things here, and this could be the start of a better relationship.

"I think we should go with him," he said aloud. "We need to see if he is telling the truth. I think he may be."

"No. You should not go with him, my husband. I fear you will not return to me."

Nonosabasut interjected in his deep rumbling voice, "It is decided. We will go with them."

He selected two additional men from the camp, and they left the wigwam to prepare for the trip downriver.

Shanadee held Kirradittii's face in her hands and looked into his eyes. With sadness in her voice, she said, "Be very careful. Don't let down your guard. Do not make my children fatherless." She reached up and straightened the blue feather in the top of his braid.

"I will be careful. I will return tonight," he replied as he cupped the back of her head in his hand and gave her a lingering kiss on the lips.

Outside in the clearing, Buchan was approached by his corporal, James Butler. "We think some of us should stay here Lieut'nt. It would show them a sign of good faith, don't you think?"

"Yes, I think you may be right, Corporal. They are sending four with us. It might make them feel better if we did that. Who did you have in mind?"

"I figured Private Bouthland and myself, sir. The lashings on our snowshoes are busted and we need to repair them anyway."

"Right, Corporal, we should be back before nightfall. Do nothing that the Indians might see as threatening. We have made huge strides with these Red Indians today. Let's make sure we don't do anything to damage that."

"I won't, Lieut'nt."

"Good. I am counting on you Corporal."

A short time later the group marched out of the camp, with Nonosabasut and Buchan walking side by side at the front of the group. Kirradittii walked at the back of the group, and the other two Beothuk were near the center of the column.

The trail was beaten down by the earlier passage of the large group as they made their way upriver, so the going was easy and the men were not hindered by the snow that had fallen. They made good time, and about an hour after leaving the Indian camp they reached the place where Buchan had left the rest of his men and the local guides.

Nonosabasut looked around the camp. The only sled there was empty and two of the Buggishaman were using it for a seat near the fire. Where were those gifts Bukn had told him would be here? Maybe this was a trick after all. He glanced at his brother who was standing on the path they had arrived on. He shrugged a little nervously. Nonosabasut decided to confront Bukn. Holding the hatchet that Bukn had presented to him back at the main camp, he pointed to it and then spread his hands, palms up.

Buchan responded by touching the hatchet with his fingers, and pointing downriver in an attempt to convey to the Indian leader that the sleds with the additional gifts had been left further downriver. He could see the Indian's confusion and realized he probably thought he was being tricked. He was in real danger of losing them and undoing all the progress they seemed to have made. It had taken him weeks to get here. He didn't want this opportunity to crumble on him. He looked around at his marines. The ones who just arrived with him were all standing. He noticed the marines sitting around the fire stirring nervously and pulling their guns across their lap. He knew seeing this giant Red Indian so close to their commander, especially with a hatchet in his hand, was unnerving them. He needed to ease the tension in his men, and quickly before this got out of hand. He held up his hand. "Take it easy, men. Everything is under control. Put your guns on the ground, and the rest of you find a seat somewhere. Let's try not to make it so obvious how outnumbered they are."

Nonosabasut watched as the Buggishaman all found a place to sit until Bukn was the only one of them left standing. At least they were less threatening now. He went to stand by his brother. "There is nothing here. He says to go further. What do you think? Is he lying?"

"This could still be a trick," Kirradittii replied suspiciously, remembering Shanadee's warnings. "Why would they have left them further downriver with all these extra men here? They could easily have brought them this far."

"I don't know."

"Perhaps he came here to get the extra men so that they can take everyone in the camp prisoners."

Nonosabasut looked at him thoughtfully. After a few moments he continued decisively, "The leader, Bukn, seems to be a good man. I will go the rest of the way."

"Not me. I am staying here until they leave, and then I'm going back to our camp with Shanadee and the children. I don't like the feel of this, Nonosabasut. There may be more men down river. With their guns they could easily kill us all."

"That is true, but they could have done that at our camp. I'm going to see this through. You take one of the men with you. I will take the other," said Nonosabasut.

"Be careful," replied Kirradittii, fearing he would never see his brother again.

Nonosabasut affectionately placed his hand on Kirradittii's shoulder, and nodded. Then he turned, and walked over to where Buchan was making preparations to continue down river.

Kirradittii threw some wood on the smoldering fire, and he and the other Indian sat on the snow covered ground watching the group as they marched into the woods and out of sight. As soon as the last marine disappeared, they jumped to their feet, kicked some snow on the fire, and set off in the direction of the camp at the Great Lake. They made good time on the beaten trail, and made it back to the Lake in less time than it had taken them to march down.

As they entered the clearing, Kirradittii noticed the two marines down by the edge of the lake, working on the lashings of their snowshoes. Nodding to them as they passed, he continued on to his wigwam in search of Shanadee.

Bouthland looked at Butler. "Isn't that two of the Indians that went with the Lieut'nt?

"Yes it is. I remember that blue feather on his head. Wonder why these two are back," he said a little nervously.

"Could be trouble," said Bouthland, "keep your eyes peeled." He watched anxiously as the two disappeared into the wigwam, immediately followed by a dozen of the tribe who had seen them enter the clearing. He could hear the sound of animated voices from inside.

"Why are you back?" asked Shanadee standing to her feet to meet Kirradittii, as he strode across the floor.

"There were no presents and there were nine more men there. I think it was a trick."

"Where is Nonosabasut?"

"He went down river with Bukn. Bukn said the rest of the presents are further down river. I think they may be gone to get more men, and then return for us."

"We need to leave the camp now! We must get the children away from here to somewhere safe."

"What about the two Buggishaman outside." We can't let them know where we are going or else they will tell the others when they get back," said Kirradittii.

"We have to kill them," said Shanadee. Heads nodded in agreement around the wigwam.

"It is the only way we will be safe," said one of the men.

"We could take them with us," said Kirradittii.

"No," replied Shanadee forcefully, "we can't take the chance."

"My sister is right," said Jaywritt. "We cannot risk taking them with us."

"There are only two of them. They wouldn't slow us down," argued Kirradittii.

"If we take them Bukn will hunt for us to get his men back. Do you want to risk the children, Kirradittii?"

"No Shanadee, you are right. We must protect the children. We must not put them in danger," said Kirradittii resignedly.

Lifting down their hathemays from the wall, Shanadee, Kirradittii, and Jaywritt each notched an arrow and stepped outside.

Hearing the slap of the frozen caribou skin against the door pole, Bouthland turned around and scrambled to his feet with alarm.

"Corporal," he shouted a warning as he hastily grabbed his rifle and started to swing it up to his shoulder. Before he could raise the gun all the way into position the first arrow penetrated deep into his chest. The gun fired harmlessly into the ground and he staggered backward, falling across Butler's gun in the snow. Butler tried desperately to pull his gun from beneath the fallen Bouthland but he quickly realized the advancing Indians would be on him before he could get it free. He leaped from the riverbank onto the ice, and began to run. Two arrows hit the ice near his running feet. The third found its mark, high in his left shoulder. Two more thudded into his chest, as he whirled around in pain. He stumbled, fell forward onto the ice and did not move again.

Jaywritt and Kirradittii dragged the lifeless body of Bouthland to where Butler had fallen on the frozen lake.

Shanadee ran back to their wigwam. She returned with her hunting knife, and removed the heads of the two marines to let their spirits escape. They carried the heads back to the shoreline where they cut two long poles, mounted them, and stuck them in the snow. This they did for all their enemies to give them easier passage into Gossett.

Kirradittii returned to their wigwam and began to pack. He was troubled. He was not sure they had done the right thing. He knew what he had seen at the first camp; no presents and many more men. Maybe he had been too hasty to agree to this. Maybe his brother was right to continue on. There was also a chance he would never see him again. Had they ruined their chance to have some kind of peace with the Buggishaman? This was getting way too confusing. He had to get the children away from here. That's all he should be thinking about right now. There would be time to worry about other things later.

His thoughts were interrupted by a commotion outside. At first he thought the Buggishaman had returned and he grabbed his hathemay and rushed through the door. Standing in the clearing was the tribe member that had accompanied Nonosabasut. He was alone. Kirradittii met him as he pushed his way through the crowd.

"Why did you leave?" he asked him with alarm, as they came face to face. "Where is my brother?"

"I saw no point in going on, so I ran off at the first chance. Nonosabasut is still with the Buggishaman. I think they were almost at the second camp when I left."

"Is he alright?" pressed Kirradittii.

"Yes."

"Did he give you instructions?"

"No. I just ran."

"Did the Buggishaman shoot at you when you ran?"

"No."

"Did any of them follow you?"

"I don't think so, but I can't be sure."

"Listen everyone," Kirradittii shouted, "take only what you can carry. We are leaving now before the Buggishaman can return."

Before long the whole group was strung out in a line across the ice. Under the last dying rays of the setting sun, they crossed to the north side of the Great Lake. There at the shoreline they left the head of one of the marines mounted on the long pole.

It began to snow again.

"We must cover our tracks from here," Kirradittii said to Jaywritt.

With the help of several men they swept the snow clean in all directions with spruce boughs. The fresh falling snow soon spread a clean blanket over the sweeping. It was as though no one had passed that way. The long pole with the Buggishaman's head was the only sign that anyone had been there.

The frightened Beothuk continued to follow the shoreline of the Great Lake westward into the night. They reached the second encampment of the tribe around midnight. Rousing them from sleep, they explained what had happened.

While Shanadee was relating the events, Kirradittii talked quietly with Jaywritt.

"I think we should stay here for the night."

"Are you sure it is safe to stop now?"

"They would not be able to follow us in the dark, if they are following us at all."

"Are you having second thoughts Kirradittii?"

"Yes, I'm no longer sure that we did the right thing. I think we may have been too hasty."

"You were the one who told us it may have been a trick."

"I know, but I've had more time to think about it."

"And, what do you think now?"

"It doesn't make sense. If they wanted to kill us they would have done it earlier. They didn't need more men and more guns to do that. Why would they have spent so much time with us and given us the presents?"

"We have only ever seen trickery and violence from the Buggishaman. Why should we have expected different this time?"

"I don't know, Jaywritt. It's just that Bukn seemed different. Perhaps they are not all bad. Nonosabasut seemed to bond with him."

"You may be right, but there is no going back now. What is done is done."

In the morning they continued west, accompanied by the three women, four men, and six children from the second encampment. After a while they turned away from the Great Lake and travelled deeper into the country. In the middle of the day they stopped and set up a temporary camp. They felt they were far enough away from the Lake to be safe.

Kirradittii also wanted to stop to give Nonosabasut a chance to catch up. He still held out hope that his brother was alive even though Shanadee and Jaywritt did not share his optimism.

On the second day Nonosabasut walked into camp. Kirradittii ran to meet him, and wrapped his arms around him in a bear hug.

"I thought I would not see you again, my brother," he said excitedly.

Nonosabasut pushed him out to arm's length and said, "I'm fine, Kirradittii. Tell me what happened back at camp?"

In a few short words, Kirradittii told him what had happened and why they ran. Nonosabasut shook his head sadly. "It was no trick, brother. The presents were at the second camp. Bukn is an honorable man."

With a sinking feeling in his heart, Kirradittii knew they had made the wrong decision in not taking the two marines with them. The Buggishaman, Bukn, had opened a door to them, and they had slammed it shut in his face. Their action had destroyed any possibility for peace for many years to come. He looked into Nonosabasut's eyes, and with sadness in his voice said, "I think we made a bad mistake, brother."

Nonosabasut nodded grimily. "It is done now," he said. "We cannot go back and change it."

"What did Bukn do when he saw the bodies? How did you escape?"

"We did not discover them the first day we returned. It was late evening by the time we got there. I knew something was wrong because the camp was deserted. I told Bukn the tribe had moved on to another camp. I think he was suspicious because he kept guards out all night while we slept in the empty wigwams."

"In the morning the bodies were spotted on the ice. When I saw what had happened, I ran into the woods. No one shot at me. Even then they could have killed me, but I don't think Bukn would let them."

"What should we do now?" asked Kirradittii. By this time everyone at the camp had gathered around their chief. They were waiting anxiously to hear his words. They needed someone to tell them what to do.

"I don't think they will follow us," he began in his deep rumbling voice, "but they may. We must go. We must warn the camp at the other end of the Lake. Let us get ready."

The tribe members nodded in agreement. They wanted to be as far from the Buggishaman as possible now. They would want revenge for this.

The group quickly dispersed, and soon had their families repacked and ready to travel. They crossed over the frozen lake to the south side, and marched through the day to the third encampment.

On arriving at the camp, they related everything that had happened to the small group that lived there. The next day they abandoned the camp and the whole tribe left and retired to a remote part of the woods, well inland from the shoreline of the Great Lake. There they built six new wigwams and spent the winter in isolation and safety.

Chapter 13
1813
Into the River

Nonosabasut worried too much. He knew it was true, and so did everyone else it seemed. Just yesterday his brother had said to him, "If you worry so much about tomorrow you will not live today." Kirradittii was probably right. Ever since the incident with Bukn things hadn't been right. He knew that what had happened that day had probably sealed their fate. The man had extended the hand of friendship and they had cut it off. The Buggishaman would not forgive them for killing their men, no matter what the reason for doing it.

The tribe had become divided over it, and in the last two years many of them drifted away in small groups. Most of these groups remained in the interior, away from the coast, avoiding all contact with the Buggishaman. Despite this, the size of the tribe continued to decline.

It was often a struggle for the smaller groups. They didn't have the help that came with being part of a larger community. Many succumbed to sickness and starvation, unable to gather and store enough supplies to see them through the harsh winters.

Nonosabasut often received reports of these tragedies, and he knew somehow he had to bring the people back to the Great Lake. He believed their survival as a nation depended on it, although he wondered at times if their numbers were already too small to make it. He supposed they numbered fifty or less by now. He knew it wasn't much of a base to build on.

In a few months he would celebrate his 40th year. If he was going to do something for the tribe he needed to do it soon.

"Lost in thought again brother?"

He had been so preoccupied with his thoughts he hadn't even heard Kirradittii come up behind him.

Kirradittii sat next to him, his feet dangling over the grassy bank. For a while he did not say anything. He just sat there quietly gazing out over the lake, absentmindedly twirling a new blue jay tail feather between his fingers. He is so much more relaxed than me thought Nonosabasut. Why is it left to me to carry the load all the time?

"So have you given it any more thought?" said Nonosabasut, breaking the prolonged silence.

"Not a lot."

"You do think it is the right thing to do, don't you?"

"Yes Nonosabasut, I think it would be best for all of us to be together again, but you can't do it singlehandedly. You can't force people to come back here. They will only come if they want to."

"I know that. I just feel responsible, somehow."

"Listen brother, you are chief when we are all together here. If people want to live somewhere else, then that is up to them. You are only responsible for them when they choose to live here."

"It's not that simple Kirradittii," he said softly.

"Isn't it? I think maybe it is."

"The tribe is disappearing. Soon there will be no one left. That is why we need to all be together… to help each other. I think it is the only way we will survive."

"You worry too much! I see you watching Demasduit," he said without pausing.

Without looking at Kirradittii, Nonosabasut replied, "I watch many people."

"But, I think this is different."

"Maybe it is."

"Shanadee says she is a good woman."

"What do you say?"

"I must agree with my wife," Kirradittii laughed.

"Yes, I think you must," Nonosabasut smiled back at him.

"We think it is time you found yourself a wife. Where did you first see her?"

"She was at the third camp. I first saw her the night we ran from Bukn."

"Yes, they were a small group. I remember seeing her then as well."

"I have asked her family to join us when we move down river next week."

"This I know, my brother. She told Shanadee today."

"So they have agreed to come with us?"

"Yes."

"Good."

Together the two families moved down the Great River, about four days travel from the Great Lake. They built a new mamateek on the river bank at a strategic place where they could see the river in both directions. Three days after arriving they were joined by two other families and two more mamateeks were built in the small clearing.

The ice had broken up and disappeared downstream. The days were growing longer. Warm air blew softly through the valley, heralding the new life brought by the onset of spring.

It was in this quiet setting that Nonosabasut took Demasduit for his bride. That night, after the celebration feast ended, she moved into the mamateek with Nonosabasut, and Shanadee and her family.

The long days of summer were spent finding and storing food for the winter. Much of their foraging was done under the cover of darkness while the Buggishaman was sleeping.

A short hike downriver, several wasemook fishermen had built weirs to corral the fish as they swam upriver to their spawning grounds. Nonosabasut, Kirradittii and Jaywritt carried out regular visits to these sites, always after the sun had gone down. It was during one of these ventures that Shanadee came close to losing her husband.

The three men had left camp just as the scarlet sun was melting into the surrounding hills. They were all carrying their long spears in their hands and had baskets slung over their shoulders to bring home their catch.

As they neared the first weir, Nonosabasut stopped, and in his lowest whisper said, "We will go on to the next fisherman's weir."

"That's further downriver. Why not take from this one?" asked Jaywritt. "We are here now."

"We took from this one last time," replied Nonosabasut. "If we continue to take from the same place, it will be noticed. That will only bring trouble on our families."

"I agree," said Kirradittii, "let's not bring more trouble on our families. It's been a good summer so far. Let's not do anything to spoil that."

"All right," said Jaywritt, reluctantly giving in. "Let's go."

By the time they approached the second fishing station, the daylight had been almost completely overtaken by the encroaching night. Over the small wooden tilt, wispy trails of smoke could be seen, framed against the dark tree covered slope of the hills behind it. The full moon had already begun its slow ascent into a cloudless, starlit sky.

The three men crouched behind a stand of evergreen, watching the tilt. Through the single small window they could see the silhouette of the fisherman as he moved around inside.

"It looks like he is alone," murmured Jaywritt.

"One Buggishaman with a gun is more dangerous than all of us," stated Nonosabasut matter-of-factly.

He will be asleep soon," whispered Kirradittii. "We should wait."

They sat on the ground in companionable silence, and patiently waited until the light finally flickered out in the window.

Cautiously, they crept out onto the wooden weir, keeping an eye on the dark tilt nearby. The full moon, now high overhead, illuminated the water, making it easy to see the wasemook as they milled around inside the weir. It made it easy to spear the fish. It also made it much easier for them to be seen out on the river. They were all very conscious of how exposed they were and kept glancing at the tilt as they worked.

It was the moon that was almost their undoing.

Nonosabasut was kneeling on the riverbank, placing his last catch in his basket, when the door of the shack burst open, swinging against the wall with a loud crash. For an instant Nonosabasut froze in surprise. The shouting figure running across the grass toward him was clad in white long johns and brandishing a long rifle. Finally realizing the danger he was in, Nonosabasut scrambled to his feet knocking over the basket and spilling the fish on the ground. He bolted toward the woods and quickly disappeared in the trees.

The fisherman immediately turned his attention to the two out on the weir. They were stranded with no way to escape. He grinned as he saw their plight.

Running toward the weir, he raised the rifle and fired. The shot went wide, but was enough to inspire the panic stricken Indians to leap into the wildly rushing water.

Jaywritt's entry was smooth, Kirradittii's was not. Forced to choose between being shot or drowned, he reluctantly chose the latter, reasoning it might be the easier way to die. Now that his feet were no longer planted firmly on the wooden weir, he quickly began to rethink the wisdom of his decision. The cold rushing river was doing its best to drown him, and there really wasn't any contest. Each time his head bobbed above the surface of the rushing water, he took great gasps of air, but as soon as he was submerged again the panic took control and he gulped down water to replace the escaping air.

The river was much stronger than him and it was winning.

He was under the water more than he was out. He was swallowing more water than air.

His panicked flailing had exhausted him and he knew his strength was finished.

Vaguely he heard someone yelling to Shanadee.

Curiously he looked around and sheepishly realized it was him. He wondered what she was doing right now.

He felt too tired to stay awake.

Then he bumped against something in the dark and instinctively grabbed on.

Jaywritt had seen Kirradittii splash into the water. He knew his brother-in-law couldn't swim, and he would have to reach him quickly if he was to have any chance at all. The moonlight turned the rippling surface of the water gray-silver, and he could see the dark form of Kirradittii silhouetted against it. He was flailing around, just downstream. The swift river current was carrying him along close to the shore.

Jaywritt struck out in strong, powerful strokes, pulling himself toward the shoreline, letting the current carry him down river as he swam. Ahead of them he saw a tall uprooted birch tree had fallen over and was sticking out into the river. He watched the tree shift as the rushing water carried Kirradittii into its branches. Jaywritt grabbed the tip of the tree as he was slipping by, and pulled himself along the trunk to where Kirradittii had locked his arms in a death grip. Bracing against the current, he planted his feet firmly on the slippery riverbed and stood up. The water only reached halfway up his chest.

Looking into Kirradittii's fear crazed eyes he said, "Push your feet down. You can stand on the bottom here."

Kirradittii stared back at him and shook his head vehemently, coughing water out of his sodden lungs.

"The Buggishaman could be here any minute. Do you want to get shot?" Jaywritt argued, trying to get Kirradittii to focus.

Kirradittii anxiously glanced upriver. He really didn't like either of the options. He closed his eyes tightly, and gripped the tree trunk a little tighter.

"Do you want to see Shanadee again?" Jaywritt tried a different tact.

In the soft moonlight, Jaywritt watched Kirradittii's eyes slowly open and focus on him. "I can't move," he whispered hoarsely. "I can't let go."

Jaywritt noticed movement in the trees a little upriver from them. "Be quiet," he whispered to Kirradittii. "Someone is coming."

Jaywritt held a branch of the tree and sank lower in the water until only his head was above the surface. Kirradittii had closed his eyes again.

Jaywritt watched the dark figure slowly move along the riverbank. From the movements he could tell the figure was searching for them. It was too dark to tell for sure, but he thought that maybe it was Nonosabasut, and not the Buggishaman.

The closer the shadowy figure got the surer he became. He whistled a night bird call and saw the figure freeze, and then turn and look in his direction. From the darkness he heard the answer.

He pushed himself to a standing position and called softly. "Over here, Nonosabasut."

Nonosabasut ran the rest of the way along the bank to the downed tree.

"What's wrong with Kirradittii?"

"He can't let go. Come out here and help me get him ashore."

"Is he hurt?" asked Nonosabasut, as he waded into the water.

"I don't think so. Just scared out of his mind! Help me get his feet on the river bottom. He won't believe he can stand up here."

Jaywritt moved behind Kirradittii to help break the effect of the current, and Nonosabasut ducked under the dark water. He grabbed Kirradittii's flailing feet, and pulled them down until he could feel the solid river bottom underneath him. Breaking the surface again Nonosabasut placed his huge hands over Kirradittii's, and slowly forced open his fingers, one at a time. Kirradittii now locked his fingers around his brother's wrists.

Together, Nonosabasut and Jaywritt coaxed him towards the shore, until they were out of the water. Kirradittii collapsed to his knees on the riverbank in relief. He was grinning widely at his two rescuers.

"You saved my life!" was all he could get out before he was overcome with spasms of uncontrollable laughter. The other two sat on the ground and were quickly infected with Kirradittii's mirth, until the night air rang with the sound of their laughter.

Jaywritt was the first to remember the Buggishaman. "We'd better keep the noise down he sputtered through his laughter. He might still be out there."

The other two glanced up river, looked at Jaywritt and launched into a new fit of laughter, although a little quieter this time.

Sometime later, when their control finally returned, all three lay on the ground staring up at the dark star studded sky, still laughing quietly at the great adventure, like three young boys.

"This will be a good story, little brother," Nonosabasut chuckled.

"The children will love this tale," laughed Jaywritt.

"Shanadee will never let me live this one down."

"Neither will we!"

"And we have no fish."

Chapter 14
1818
Shanadee

Winter had to be coaxed to leave and so spring was late arriving in 1818. The long bitter winter had taken its toll on the tribe and their meager supplies had all but run out. Some tribe members had fallen victim to the harsh storms that dragged on into late April and there were fresh graves at the Great Lake.

It was now the middle of May and Shanadee and her extended family had moved down river to a summer camp much closer to the ocean. She was not totally comfortable with being this close to the Buggishaman but there had not been any incidents in the last few years and they needed to harvest food from the waters at the coast. Kirradittii had convinced her it would be safe if they stayed away from the Buggishaman settlements. She hoped he was right, but she had no intention of letting her guard down.

The warm spring winds were finally beginning to waft down from the surrounding hills, triggering the dormant trees to unfold their leaves, reaching hungrily for the warmth of the long-absent sun. As each day passed by the sun grew stronger, stretching the daylight later into the evenings.

Stepping outside the dark mamateek, Shanadee was momentarily blinded by the bright flash of sunlight that bounced off the surface of the river water. Squinting her eyes against the glare, she lifted her face toward the sky and drew in a deep breath of air, savoring the fresh smells of the awakening forest. Looking up at the cloudless sky, she knew this would be the day.

She had been planning a trip to the bird islands to harvest eggs since the last ice had melted and disappeared from the river. If they left now they should be able to get to the coast by noon.

The tribe had two sea tapaithooks that were hidden amongst the trees on a secluded beach well away from any settlements. Some of the men had used them recently, so she knew they were in good condition and not damaged by the winter freeze.

Stepping back inside the mamateek, she loudly announced her intention.

"Hey, wake up everybody! Today is a good day to gather bird eggs. Anyone want to come with me?"

Before she had finished, Ojjbawitt had thrown back his sleeping furs and leaped to his feet. Grabbing his hathemay he rushed to her side. "I'm going," he proclaimed enthusiastically, and ran out the door.

"We will go as well, mother" said Shanawdithit, indicating herself and her younger sister. Mandolee nodded and grinned at Shanadee. One of her front teeth was missing from a fall she had taken when she was younger. It gave her a lopsided smile. Shanadee could not help but smile back at her disarming grin. Before she could speak, Ojjbawitt rushed back in the door with his best friend, Dogavikt, in tow.

"Can he come, mother?" he asked in his best pleading voice, still breathing hard from his run. "His mother said he could," he rushed on, looking at his friend for confirmation. Dogavikt nodded anxiously.

Not wanting to spoil their adventure, Shanadee smiled at the two boys, and said, "Yes, he may, let's go." She held the door flap aside, and they all filed out. Before following the others through the door she smiled back at Demasduit who had been watching the whole thing from her bed.

"Be careful, Shanadee," she said sleepily. "Stay away from the Buggishaman."

"I will. We will be back after dark tomorrow," she said as she stepped through the door and let it fall shut behind her.

The two eleven year old boys walked out in front of the group. They were totally engaged in a lively conversation about the merits of the long hathemay versus the short ones they had looped over their shoulders. They talked about how someday they would bring down their first caribou with the long hathemay. Ojjbawitt proudly reminded his friend that his mother was the best shot in the tribe with the long hathemay, and she had been teaching him how to shoot. So he was going to be a great shot as well. "It just makes sense doesn't it?"

Shanadee listened to the girls walking behind her as they discussed the young men of the tribe, and who they thought would be a likely candidate for their affections.

Walking in the midst of this, Shanadee smiled contentedly. Her family was growing up in front of her, and would soon be starting their own families. This is the way life was meant to be, she thought happily. How could this day get any better!

Kirradittii and Jaywritt had left before sunup to hunt caribou. They would not likely return tonight. She enjoyed this time alone with her children. It was interesting how they were all different, she thought. Shanawdithit with her love for drawing, Mandolee filled with fears and anxiety like her father, and Ojjbawitt, full of life and promise. I wonder how their lives will unfold in the future, she thought. It will be fun to watch them grow.

The sun was high overhead when they arrived at the coast. The light wind blowing in from the ocean wasn't enough to create white caps on the waves. "It should be a good trip to the island," said Shanadee looking out over the quiet water.

"Where are the tapaithooks, Mother?" asked Ojjbawitt excitedly, wanting to get on with it.

"They are hidden over there near that pile of rocks," she replied. "Before we get one we will have lunch. It is a long trip to the island."

"Where is the island?"

"Can you see that tiny blue speck way out there?" she said pointing out to sea.

"I can't see it, Mother," replied Ojjbawitt. "All I see is water."

"I can," said Mandolee quietly. "That's way too far."

Glancing at her daughter's worried face, Shanadee replied reassuringly, "It's not as far as it looks. The water plays tricks on your eyes. It will be all right Mandolee. It's not windy, so there is nothing at all to worry about."

Her plan was for Shanawdithit to stay on shore and wait for them to return. Now she wondered if she should leave Mandolee instead. She needed the extra room in the boat, so one of them would not be going. She thought Mandolee would be better with her. She would probably be more scared staying here alone on the beach than in the tapaithook, she rationalized.

"How many paddles are there?"

"There're three, Ojjbawitt."

"Great," said Ojjbawitt, looking at his friend happily. "Now we won't have to fight each other over who gets to paddle."

Once they had finished their lunch, they moved down the beach to the pile of rocks that Shanadee had pointed out. None of them could see any sign of the boats from there. Pushing their way through the thick brush, Shanadee led them to the spot where the two tapaithooks were cleverly hidden underneath a covering of broken branches. Selecting the nearest one they pulled away the branches and dragged it out onto the beach.

"That's not very big," observed Mandolee nervously.

"It can easily carry all of us, but your sister is going to wait here for us to return. That will make more room for the eggs," her mother replied.

"Let's go," said Ojjbawitt impatiently.

"Ok," said Shanadee, "lift the tapaithook until we get it in the water. Be careful not to hit the rocks and damage the bottom."

The five of them found a place to grip the tapaithook and they lifted it and carried it across the beach into the shallow water.

"Everyone find a large flat rock to place in the bottom of the tapaithook," instructed Shanadee.

"Won't that sink it, Mother?" worried Mandolee.

"No it will help keep it from tipping," replied her mother.

As they brought her the rocks, she carefully placed them in a line along the v in the bottom of the tapaithook.

"Now there is a bunch of sods back there where the tapaithook was hidden. We need to get them to place over the rocks, so we can kneel on them."

The two boys ran up the beach to the tree line, and moments later reappeared with an armful of sods.

When these were in place, Shanawdithit held the tapaithook while they all climbed in, and then she pushed it away from the shore into deeper water.

Shanawdithit waded back to shore, picked up her food sack and stood watching them paddle away from the shoreline. Then she began following an old animal path that wound its way to the top of the hill that provided a protected headland to the small cove. From there she would have a good view of the ocean. She would be able to watch them all the way to the hazy, blue island in the distance. It would be a good place to draw them, she thought.

By the time she had climbed all the way to the top they had paddled the tapaithook out of the sheltered cove into open water. Mandolee who was kneeling in the front was the only one without a paddle. That's not surprising, thought Shanawdithit; she always finds a way to avoid work. It was a constant battle to get her younger sister to do anything. She was always busy in her imaginary world with her imaginary friends.

Shanawdithit found a comfortable spot and sat in the short brown grass where she could watch the progress of the tapaithook. The light breeze was barely enough to stir the grass that surrounded her, but it was enough to make the heat from the sun bearable. It was going to be a long afternoon. It would probably be almost dark before they returned to the beach.

She pulled a rolled sheet of birch bark and a burnt stick from her bag and arranged it on her lap to draw her family as they paddled out to sea. The warm sun on her back was making her drowsy, and she knew she had better get this done before she was overcome with the need to sleep. Although she couldn't hear from this distance, she could see by their actions the two boys were still talking. They never seemed to run out of things to talk about. She pitied her mother.

She picked up the charcoal stick and turned to see the shape of the coast to her left. Her heart leaped. Appearing round the tip of the point was the dirty white sail of a small fishing boat. The hair on the back of her neck prickled and her throat went dry with fear. Scrambling to her feet, the now forgotten birch bark slipped to the ground and tumbled end over end as the gentle wind caught it and swept it along the ground. Shanawdithit jumped up and down, waving frantically as she tried to yell a warning to her mother. At first no sound came out of her dry throat. Swallowing hard she tried again. This time she yelled at the top of her lungs. "Mother! Mother, the Buggishaman. Come back. You've got to come back!"

They can't hear me. They are too far away, she realized as the icy fingers of dread gripped her chest.

She had no way to warn them!

She kept waving her arms in the air hoping to catch their attention, but they weren't looking her way.

With a sinking feeling of despair, she watched the sailboat turn toward the tapaithook, as the men gestured excitedly in its direction.

Finally the tapaithook began to turn, but she knew it was too late. She thought she saw her mother lift her hand to her.

She dropped her arms in helpless frustration. Her nails bit into her tightly clasped hands as she watched the sailboat gain on the slow moving tapaithook.

"No!" she moaned softly. "Please no."

From the corner of her eye, Shanadee noticed Shanawdithit waving frantically atop the hill, and turned to look over her shoulder. The smile froze on her face, and a cold chill ran up her spine.

"Turn the tapaithook! We must go back", she urgently cried to the boys.

Hearing the unmistakable anxiety in her voice, they all turned and looked back. Over her shoulder they saw the dirty white sail rushing down on them. Without a word, they whirled around and dug their paddles deep into the dark water, pulling the tapaithook in the direction of the faraway beach.

Shanadee's eyes were drawn to her oldest daughter, waving and jumping up and down high atop the cliff. The distance was much too great, but she knew her first born was crying with frustration at not being able to help. With tears in her eyes, Shanadee raise her hand to her, to tell her it was alright. She saw Shanawdithit's arms fall limply to her side, and across the distance she felt their hearts connect for the last time.

Below the cliff she saw the grey moisamadrook loping along the sandy beach.

With resignation she let the paddle slip from her hand, picked up her hathemay from the bottom of the tapaithook, and arranged three arrows between her fingers. Following her lead, the boys placed their paddles on the floor, and notched arrows in their hathemays as well. Mandolee cowered down in the front of the gently rocking tapaithook, shaking with fear as they waited for the inevitable.

Shanadee knelt and calmly watched the approaching doom. She knew with a certainty they would not all make it through this. With the fingers of her right hand she gently stroked the bright blue feather that she had tucked into her belt before leaving camp. She whispered softly, "Kirradittii."

She could see that the three Buggishaman in the boat were laughing and shouting to each other, caught up in the excitement of the hunt. The one in the front of the boat and the one in the center had guns pointed in their direction. The Buggishaman in the back was steering the boat. She knew their guns would be able to reach them long before her arrows could hit the boat. All she had was her short hathemay and she would never reach the boat using that.

"Make your arrows count," she commanded. She watched with bittersweet pride, as the two boys knelt on one knee in the bottom of the tapaithook, and pulled their hathemay strings as far back as their young arms could, waiting for the Buggishaman to come close enough.

The first shot hit Ojjbawitt in the chest hurling him over the side into the water. Without looking Shanadee knew he was gone and she felt a piece of her go with him. Dogavikt's arrow fell far short of the sailboat. He bent to pick up a second arrow, as gunshot tore away his left shoulder, knocking him flat against the side of the tapaithook.

Splattered with blood Mandolee was screaming in terror at the front of the tapaithook.

Shanadee released two arrows in quick succession, before a gunshot smashed into her arm, spinning the hathemay out across the water. Looking at Mandolee cowering in the front of the tapaithook, her heart was ripped in pain. "I'm sorry.

I love you, my daughter," she whispered hoarsely, and crumpled to the floor of the tapaithook. She heard the high pitched howl from the distant beach.

From her high vantage point, Shanawdithit watched in horror as the sailboat pulled alongside, and gunshots punched holes in the fragile bark tapaithook. In seconds it was reduced to floating debris on the dark waves. Her trembling knees could no longer support her, and she collapsed in agony on the grass. Over and over she screamed their names, until she finally slid into a dark place that was devoid of all light.

Chapter 15
1819
Kirradittii

That summer was a lonely and terribly troubling time for Kirradittii. Most of his family had been taken from him in that single brutal act. Only his oldest daughter remained, and she had withdrawn into a place of sadness; a place where she even abandoned her beloved drawings. They seldom talked to each other anymore, and conversations never ventured beyond the routines of daily life.

He no longer bothered to braid his hair, and the familiar blue feather that he had worn so proudly was not there anymore. There just didn't seem any point to it now that Shanadee was gone.

His dreams were haunted by vivid pictures of the senseless slaughter, burned into his memory since that horrible first day when Shanawdithit stumbled back into camp and described what she had seen. Sleep no longer came easily for him, and when it did he often woke the rest of those sleeping around him with his moaning and pleading calls to his lost family. It was a very unhappy time and nothing seemed to help.

He spent countless days away from camp, wandering alone in the forest, trying desperately to find peace and relive the happy years he'd had with Shanadee. He traveled alone to the sea coast and searched the beaches for his family, but always returned empty handed. It seemed time might be the only healer for him, and some thought maybe even time would not allow him to find his way back.

His brother and Demasduit did their best to help both him and Shanawdithit move past the crippling tragedy, but everything they did seemed to be in vain. Sometimes Nonosabasut worried that his younger brother was not going to make it, and might someday take the easy way out.

It had taken all of Nonosabasut's power of persuasion to convince Kirradittii to return to the winter camp at the Great Lake, but in the end he agreed and he and Shanawdithit followed the main group, about a half day behind.

Shanawdithit had settled into the routine at the winter camp and she had begun to draw again. Kirradittii on the other hand was showing no signs of getting past the loss. Then came the birth of Nonosabasut and Demasduit's first child.

All of a sudden Kirradittii found a new focus, and he showered his little niece with attention. Their wigwam was once again filled with the musical sounds of a newborn baby's cry. Even though at times it served as a reminder of his missing children, the birth seemed to mark a new beginning for the wigwam, and the soft gurgling sounds were a healing balm slowly pushing back the darkness that had settled so heavily upon the family.

It was now March, and there were signs the spring thaw would soon be here. The baby was a little over two weeks old. Inside Nonosabasut's wigwam, the family was enjoying the newness of the child when suddenly the reverie was shattered by the chilling sound of a gunshot echoing through the quiet morning air. It was the sound that could only mean one thing, the Buggishaman were here again. That sound, like no other, immediately struck terror in the hearts of the Beothuk.

The whole tribe poured from their wigwams and ran for the protection of the woods, looking for somewhere to hide from the evil that had descended on them once again.

"Here, let me take her," said Nonosabasut, as he scooped his newborn daughter from Demasduit's arms. "It will be easier for you to run if I carry her."

He tenderly cradled the tiny bundle in his arms, turned, and ran to the edge of the woods where the others had disappeared into the trees. At the tree line he stopped and looked back at his struggling wife, who was still a long way from the safety of the trees. She was not yet fully recovered from the childbirth and was running in faltering spurts. He could see the pain and fear on her face as she determinedly pushed herself to keep going.

"Hurry," he yelled, looking at the Buggishaman who were gaining on her. She was wading through the deep snow and they were wearing snowshoes. With a sinking heart he knew she would not be able to outrun them.

The lead runner caught her long before she reached the safety of the woods. She stumbled and fell as he grabbed her from behind. He held her down in the snow as she struggled and screamed to Nonosabasut for help.

As if a spear was thrust through his chest, Nonosabasut's heart was pierced by the pleading screams for help from his struggling wife. That was the mother of his child back there and he knew he had to help her. Whatever her fate he would share it. Through the trees he could see Shanawdithit watching him. He held out the baby to her and she came to him. She took the little bundle from his arms and ran with it back into the safety of the woods.

Nonosabasut snapped off a small branch from a spruce tree. Holding it over his head in what he hoped they would recognize as a peace sign, he walked back onto the snow covered ice and into the midst of the ten armed men who had circled his wife.

Looking around the group, he recognized old John Peyton and he was scared. He had encountered him in previous raids, and knew he had no reservations about killing Beothuk.

"Let her go!" he shouted. "She is my wife," he continued in his deep rumbling voice, motioning towards Demasduit.

"What's he saying?"

"I don't know, but be careful. He's a big bugger."

"Look at that ugly scar across his face. He's been in a fight before."

"I think he intends to take her back."

"He's not getting her. She is coming with us," growled Peyton. "The Governor wants us to capture one of them and we are taking her. Keep an eye on him," he said to the other men standing around them with their guns at the ready. "Be careful where you shoot. Don't hit any of us."

Ignoring the guns, Nonosabasut reached down and grabbed the outstretched hand of Demasduit and tried to pull her away from her captors. Looking into her tear filled eyes he said, "Don't be afraid, Demasduit. I will get you out of this."

Someone shoved him from behind and he stumbled into Peyton. Grabbing at the old man to keep from falling, he held him by the shoulders and then shook him, shouting into his face. "I only want to take my wife. Leave us alone."

"Help me," yelled Peyton. "Get this filthy Indian off me! Don't just stand there men. Can't you see he's trying to kill me?"

"Shoot him!" someone yelled.

"Get him off Mr. Peyton!"

"Shoot. Now!"

Kirradittii left the cover of the trees and started toward the shouting, milling group.

"I have to help Demasduit and my brother," he shouted over his shoulder to Shanawdithit.

He had almost reached the group, when a gun roared and he watched his brother stumble to his knees, and then tumble face first in the snow.

Demasduit screamed hysterically, "You have killed him you devils. You have killed my husband. No. Please no!" She crawled to him and rolled him from his side unto his back. Sobbing wildly she lay her head on his chest and let her tears mingle with the blood that stained the front of his cloak.

Kirradittii stood facing them for a moment, not fully registering what had just happened there on the ice in front of him. It took him a few seconds to reach the conclusion that he would be next and there was nothing he could do to help either his brother or Demasduit. He turned and ran toward the woods where Shanawdithit and the rest of the tribe were hiding. It wasn't far. He was going to make it.

"Kill the other one. He's getting away," the old man shouted. "Shoot. Shoot him!"

The shot ripped into his back, driving the air from his lungs and pitching him forward into the soft white snow. He saw

Shanawdithit watching behind a thick spruce tree. She was clutching his brother's newborn against her chest. The searing pain ran up his back in rolling waves and he could no longer see clearly. "Shanadee," he whispered hoarsely, as the light faded away.

Later that afternoon Jaywritt and Langnon, Demasduit's brother, set out to track the group of Buggishaman, hoping to be able to free Demasduit. The group left a wide trail of trampled snow making it easy to follow and the beaten path allowed Jaywritt and Langnon to travel fast. They soon caught up with the Buggishaman.

The group was crossing the ice on a small pond.

"Do you see her?" asked Langnon.

"I think so," replied Jaywritt. "Isn't that her on the sled, there in the middle of the group?"

"Yes, I think it might be. Your eyes are better than mine, Jaywritt. Is she moving?"

"It looks like she might be telling them what to do. She's waving her arms about."

"She must be alive then. We should try to get closer."

"Do you see those two keeping back from the others?"

"Yes. What are they up to?"

"They are guards. See how they keep looking back along the trail? See how they are keeping their guns ready?"

"They are not going to let us anywhere near my sister, are they?"

"No, they're not. There is no chance of us rescuing her from this large a group. They seem to be treating her well. We have to let her go."

"I can't just let her go without trying."

"You have no choice. They will kill you. Haven't we had enough of that today?"

"Do you think she will survive?"

"They are not going to kill her. If they were, they would have done that already."

"I guess you're right."

"Let's go back."

"Yes, let's go."

The late evening shadows had arrived by the time Jaywritt and Langnon made it back to the camp. There they discovered the tribe had already made preparations to bury their chief and his brother.

Just a little way from the main camp they found the small wooden hut that had been built to store the bodies until the ground thawed and a more permanent burial could be performed. Jaywritt crawled inside to inspect the work. The walls had been made by lacing together sticks, some of which they had managed to hammer into the frozen ground. Jaywritt tugged on the fishing line and it seemed strong enough to hold everything together. He gently pushed against the rack suspended above the ground by four posts. It seemed steady enough, so he backed out of the low door on his knees. He was satisfied the hut would protect the bodies of his two best friends until summer. Then he would have something better built for them.

Kneeling there in the snow, the weight of the loss seemed to be a burden he might not be able to carry. They were not only family but his best friends. Memories of their good times flooded his mind and trickled from the corners of his eyes as tears. He felt Langnon's hand squeeze his shoulder.

"They were good men, Jaywritt. We have had much taken from us today."

Early the next morning the bodies of the two brothers were brought to the hut and placed on the rack. Next to the bodies they arranged the necessary tools for their journey across the river to Gossett.

Shanawdithit applied a fresh coat of odemet to one of her mother's hathemays and placed it next to Kirradittii. She braided his unruly hair and arranged a fresh blue jay feather at just the angle he had always worn it. Next to his hand she placed a bark container in which she inserted a rolled up drawing of all the members of the family.

After the ceremony, Shanawdithit brought the tiny newborn back to Nonosabasut's wigwam. It had not fed since Demasduit had been taken, and there was no other mother in the tribe who could nurse it. There was nothing Shanawdithit could do except hold the weakened baby until it stopped crying. Through her tears she sang softly to it all through the night until, in the early dawn, it stopped whimpering and she felt its spirit leave. She coated the little body with odemet, wrapped it, and placed it in the burial hut next to Nonosabasut.

She went back to the wigwam, sat next to the fire and cried. Her uncle Jaywritt, his wife Doodlebewshet, and their daughter and son, were all that remained of the family. Their wigwam felt empty. The only thing left to fill it were the memories.

There were now only thirty one of them left in the three wigwams at the lake. She knew there wasn't much chance of them surviving. She remembered how her uncle Nonosabasut had worried about that, and that was when there were almost a hundred of them. Yet, life had to go on.

Chapter 16
1819
Preduc

During the rest of that summer and fall Shanawdithit found herself spending more and more time with Preduc, who lived with his mother and little sister in the wigwam next to hers. He was almost the same age as her, and now the tribe was so small it seemed natural they pair up to hunt and gather food. They had become close friends, and seldom would you see one around the camp without the other. It was rumored there would be a wedding in the winter.

She had heard the whispered rumors, and maybe they were right, she thought. Preduc had helped her through her worst time. He had been there when she needed to talk about her lost family, and he had also been there when she didn't want to talk at all. She had been able to lean on his strength through that dark time. Even in the midst of all the terrible sadness he had been able to make her feel better. She wondered why she hadn't noticed him before.

Maybe it was because he didn't stand out. He was almost the same height as her, he had been born the same year, and he was soft spoken just like her. He cropped his hair just above the shoulder. That was short for a Beothuk, but she liked it.

Maybe the fact that he didn't stand out is what drew him to her in the first place. Whatever it was she wasn't sure. She just knew she liked spending time with him.

They were walking side by side on a path near the camp. The sun had begun sliding out of sight behind the distant hills. Already it was getting darker here in the woods. Suddenly Preduc stopped and pointed excitedly.

"Look over there," he whispered.

Turning in the direction he was pointing, Shanawdithit could just make out a small group of caribou grazing on the snow-covered bog. In the fading light it was difficult to tell, but she thought she could see six of them in the group.

"I see them," she replied. "How many are there?"

"I count six."

"That is what I thought. Should we get our bows?"

"No, it's too late now. It will be dark in a few minutes."

"They probably won't go far tonight anyway."

"We'll leave at first light," announced Preduc.

"It will be good to get fresh meat for the camp."

Slipping his hand in hers, he smiled happily as they strolled back to the clearing. With his fingers he lightly massaged the white scar on the top of her hand. She had already explained how she had been shot by the Buggishaman, and he had developed the habit of gently massaging it when they held hands. He hoped they did a lot more of that in the coming days. It felt good.

She didn't mind, in fact, she liked to feel his fingers as they gently kneaded the scar tissue.

At the door to her wigwam, he bent and kissed her softly on the lips before she pulled back the caribou skins and disappeared inside.

When Shanawdithit stepped outside the next morning, the light was only just beginning to filter into the gray overcast sky. Preduc was already standing in front of his family's wigwam, patiently waiting for her.

His face lit with a broad smile as he saw her emerge from the dark wigwam.

The wind had risen overnight, and the cold gusts bit all the way through the thick furs she was wearing. She pulled them a little tighter around her as she walked to his wigwam.

"I see you Preduc," she said cheerfully, her breath sending a swirling cloud of steam around her head when she spoke.

"I see you Shanawdithit," he smiled. "Are you ready to hunt?"

"I am. Let's go find those caribou."

"Are you cold?"

"No, I'm fine."

Preduc took the lead, following the path along the river bank. The ponds had only recently frozen over, and the river still had sections of open water, so they stayed off the ice. He carried his long hathemay over his left shoulder, next to a quiver of arrows. Shanawdithit followed close behind with an empty sack slung over her shoulder. They would use this later to bring the caribou organs back to camp. Light snow was falling from a dark menacing sky, heavy with the threat of a storm. The wind swirled and tossed the snowflakes around them as they walked along the path.

Today Shanawdithit felt happy. Spending time with Preduc always helped fill the huge vacant emptiness inside her that had once been filled with her family. She moved up to walk side by side with him where the path widened out. From the corner of her eye, she watched the strong lines of his dark red face as he talked. He is a beautiful Indian, she thought. He reminds me of my father. He will make a good husband.

A gust of chilling wind, swept up from the river, caused her to shiver uncontrollably. Looking up at the dark sky she said, "We have to hurry, or we will not get back to camp before the storm hits."

"It's alright," replied Preduc confidently. "We are close now. See, the tracks are not completely covered with snow. They can't be very far ahead."

"There," said Shanawdithit, excitedly pointing through the trees.

Preduc saw them at the same instant, and slipped the hathemay from his shoulder. "There are only three of them," he whispered quietly.

"The others must be further in the woods," Shanawdithit replied.

"Probably around here somewhere."

"Shoot the small doe," Shanawdithit said, pointing at the closest animal.

"Why did you pick that one?"

"We won't be able to carry the bigger ones if we are caught in the storm."

"Luckily, we are down wind. They have no idea we are here. I'm going to have to get closer with this wind. It will blow the arrow way off course."

The three animals were standing underneath a stand of large evergreens, sheltering from the whipping wind and snow.

Preduc notched an arrow in the hathemay. He bent low and edged closer to his unsuspecting prey. Shanawdithit stood motionless, watching his stealthy progress through the trees. She enjoyed this part of the hunt, although sometimes she found herself rooting for the animals. She knew they needed the meat for the camp, but the caribou looked so beautiful. She would much rather draw them on sheets of birch rind.

The rumbling in her stomach brought her back to the present, and she tensed slightly as she watched Preduc draw the hathemay string tight. He pulled the arrow until it touched his cheek and released it with a sharp twang. It flew straight and true and pierced the doe through the chest, penetrating its heart. The stricken animal tried to follow the other two as they raced away through the trees, but fell to its knees within a few steps.

Preduc was on it in seconds. He mercifully dispensed the caribou with his knife. He knew how much Shanawdithit hated to see animals suffer.

Quickly he cleaned and carved up the meat. Removing the heart, liver, kidneys and the stomach he placed them in the sack Shanawdithit had brought. The weather was getting much worse and there was no time to eat the liver and celebrate the kill as was their custom. He handed her the bag and his hathemay, and then slung the caribou over his shoulders. Leading the way, he headed back towards the frozen river.

By now the snow was heavy and the wind drove it into their faces like tiny needles. They had to bow their heads to walk into the bitterly cold wind.

"We will walk on the ice", shouted Preduc over his shoulder. "It is not as sheltered as the trees, but we will go faster. We need to get back to camp and get out of this storm."

Shanawdithit nodded silently, and trudged along behind him. The large round eyes of the caribou seemed to watch her, as its lifeless head swung back and forth on Preduc's back with each step he took. For most of the time she kept her head down, protecting her eyes from the driving snow. She just concentrated on following his footprints in the snow. She clung to the heavy bag on her shoulder with both hands. Occasionally she would stop and shift the load to her other shoulder. She would then have to hurry to catch up with Preduc, who kept up a steady pace across the snow covered ice.

The howling wind made conversation impossible. She raised her head to check their progress. Shielding her eyes with her hand she peered into the swirling snow. Preduc was barely visible, even though he was just a few steps ahead. The sack was cutting into her shoulder so she stopped to shift her load again. It seemed to be getting heavier with every step. Looking around her she saw the familiar snow covered shape of the huge boulder that marked the last bend in the river before their camp. With relief she realized they were almost home. It would be good to get out of this storm and into the shelter of the warm wigwam. They had to cross the river here. Preduc had kept going and was ahead of her again. Looking through the fingers of the hand she held in front of her eyes she saw him turn and wave her on. She returned the gesture with her free hand and then lifted the sack to her other shoulder and gripped the bag with both hands again. Out on the ice, near the middle of the river, she saw Preduc turn back into the wind, take a step and disappear.

Screaming in horror, she let the bag slide from her shoulder, and began to run. Where Preduc had been, she saw only dark rushing water. On the edge of the ice lay the caribou carcass. As she got closer, it was drawn into the water by the current and swept away underneath the ice.

In despair she stopped running, knowing she could go no closer to the open water. Frantically she looked around her for some sign of Preduc, but her only companions were the howling wind and driving snow. Slowly she sank to her knees on the snow covered ice, and let the bitter anguish of her sorrow take control.

She cried that day, not just for Preduc, but for the many in her family that had been so violently taken from her. She cried for her people who were disappearing around her. She cried because the future had no place for them. Destiny had brought them to a place where survival as a people was no longer possible.

The falling snow had completely covered her curled body, so that she was just another mound of fresh snow on the surface of the river ice, indistinguishable from any other. Her tortured mind had somehow found sleep.

It was the angry snarling that had brought her back. Lifting her head, she brushed away the snow, and looked down river. The storm had blown itself out. The raging wind that had drowned out all other sound had moved on and left a quiet stillness over the land.

Two large moisamadrook were digging in the snow where she had dropped the bag and Preduc's hathemay. As she pushed to her feet, they turned and stared at her across the ice. Realizing she had no weapon other than the knife at her side, she slowly backed away towards the tree line. One of the moisamadrook, overcome with the scent of fresh meat, returned to frantically digging out the prize. The other moved a couple of steps in her direction, continuing to watch her with wary yellow eyes, a low growl rattling from deep in its throat.

Step by antagonizing step, Shanawdithit backed toward the trees.

The digger yelped in victory as he ripped a piece of the bag from the frozen snow. Not wanting to miss out on his share, the other moisamadrook tore its gaze from the retreating figure, whirled and rushed into the feast. Shanawdithit turned and walked into the woods, breaking into a run as soon as she was out of sight of the pair.

Chapter 17
1820
DEMASDUIT

There were so few of them now they were more like a band, not a tribe, and certainly not a nation. Their winter camp was no longer used at Great Lake. There didn't seem to be any point in going all the way there. It used to be for safety, protection in numbers, that sort of thing. Their numbers were so small now there was little or no protection regardless of where they camped.

Nevertheless he wasn't ready to give up yet. The site they selected was inland from the river about half a day downriver from the Lake. It was close enough so that it didn't take long to reach the river, but deep enough in the woods to avoid contact with the Buggishaman.

He shared his wigwam with his wife Doodlebewshet, their son Aaduth, their daughter Linguitt, and his niece Shanawdithit. There were twelve other Beothuk living in the other two wigwams at the camp. He did not know of any other Beothuk living on the island and he was pretty certain they were all that remained.

All that he had left were the stories handed down through the generations past. They were stories that his sister, Shanadee, had told him when he was just a boy. They were the same stories that she had been told by their father many years ago.

The proud and gentle nation of his ancestors that had once covered much of the island, and numbered in the thousands, had been brought down to a mere seventeen tribe members. There was no hope for survival. Only the memories were left now; the good memories of growing up with his older sister in better times. But even those memories were tainted with all the tragedies that had been dealt his family by the Buggishaman.

Those were the thoughts that occupied his mind as he and Aaduth followed the fresh caribou tracks through the snowy woods. They had tracked the two animals to the point where they had crossed the frozen river and were now following them on the path that paralleled the river.

Jaywritt, who was in the lead, suddenly grabbed his son by the arm and pulled him down on his knees in the soft snow. He put his finger to his lips as a warning and pointed through the trees toward the river.

"What is it, Father? Do you see the caribou?" he whispered excitedly.

"No. Look, over there on the ice. It's the Buggishaman."

Aaduth crawled through the snow to the edge of the path, and peered through the opening in the trees. There in the distance was a line of men moving up the river towards them. They were pulling several sleds. In the center of the group several of the men pulled a larger sled that carried a large wooden box. It seemed to be heavier than the other sleds.

"What are they doing?" asked Aaduth.

"I don't know, son. Whatever it is, it can't be good for us."

"Who are they?"

"They are soldiers. See their guns. I think that one in front may be Bukn."

"Are they coming back for us?"

"Maybe they are. They may want revenge for the two soldiers we killed. You go back to camp and warn the others. I will follow them and see where they go."

"What should I tell them?"

"Tell them the Buggishaman is here, and make sure they put someone on watch. They should be ready to run. Tell them not to have any fires until I get back."

"When will you be back?"

"I'm not sure. I have to see where they are going. Go now and be careful. When you cross the river be sure to cover your tracks like I taught you. We can't let them find our camp."

Jaywritt watched anxiously as his young son ran back up the path. He was just an eight year old boy who had been given a man's job. He hoped he would be alright and that he crossed the ice far enough up river so that he couldn't be spotted by the Buggishaman. He turned back to watch their progress.

The peaceful morning routine of the camp was shattered as Aaduth came running out of the woods yelling, "The Buggishaman are back."

Immediately, everyone rushed from their wigwams, heading for the protection of the woods.

"No, no," yelled Aaduth breathlessly. "They are not here. They are travelling up the river. Father sent me to warn you."

"Where is your father?" asked Doodlebewshet.

"Father is going to follow them to see what they are doing. He says they are soldiers. He thinks Bukn may be their leader."

"How many are there?" asked Shanawdithit.

"Many. There are probably twenty or more. They're pulling a sled with a large box."

Remembering what had happened almost ten years ago, Shanawdithit said, "Maybe he is bringing more presents. Uncle Nonosabasut always said he was a good man."

"Maybe he has come to kill us all," someone else said.

"We don't even know if it is Bukn."

"Should we go further into the country?"

"Don't put anything on the fires to make them smoke. Let them die out themselves."

"Father said to wait here and stay hidden until he comes back," interjected Aaduth. "I will go back to the edge of the river and keep watch."

"Be careful, my son," said Doodlebewshet. Don't take any chances with the Buggishaman. Make sure they don't see you."

"I will be careful mother," he replied as he turned and walked back into the woods.

Later that evening just before the evening shadows were completely smothered by the fast approaching night, Jaywritt and Aaduth arrived back in camp together. The relieved tribe members anxiously crowded into Jaywritt's wigwam to find out what he had seen.

Jaywritt looked around his home. He was struck by the bitter irony of what he was seeing. He had just tracked the Buggishaman who, a couple of years ago, probably could have given them the best chance at survival, and here they were now, with the entire tribe in this small wigwam. And the troubling thing was, there was still plenty of room to sit down.

"Tell us what happened."

"Are we safe here?"

Jaywritt held up his hands and the little group quickly fell silent.

"I followed the Buggishaman up river to our old camp at the Great Lake," he began. "There were 20 soldiers in the group. They were pulling several sleds. One of the sleds had a large covered box."

"Did you find out what was in the box?"

"Was Bukn the leader?" asked Shanawdithit.

"Yes he was. I stayed hidden and watched them from the woods, but I was close enough to see it was him."

"What did they do at the camp?"

"First they looked around and searched the empty wigwams."

"They were looking for us."

"It is good we did not go there this winter," said Jaywritt.

"Yes it is good," someone agreed.

Jaywritt continued. "They unloaded the big box and everything from another one of the sleds. Then they left and went back down river."

"Did you check the box?"

"First I followed them for a while to make sure they had left. When I was sure they weren't coming back, I went back to the camp. They left a pile of blankets and things next to the box. They were presents like the last time. I used one of the hatchets to open the cover." He patted the shiny new hatchet tucked into his belt.

"Tell us what you saw, Jaywritt."

"Inside the box I found the body of Demasduit."

"No!" gasped one of the women.

"She must have died with the Buggishaman."

"Maybe they killed her. Did you see signs of that?"

"No." replied Jaywritt. "I could see no marks on her."

"Why would they bring her home?"

"It must have been Bukn's doing. Uncle Nonosabasut always said he was a good man," said Shanawdithit.

"We must go and bury Demasduit with Nonosabasut and their daughter."

"We will go tomorrow," said Jaywritt. "She is not ready to cross over. They washed all the odemet from her skin. We need to prepare her for the journey."

Chapter 18
1823
Final Days

April was one of her favorite months. It had always been that way. She loved how it brought with it so many changes: the melting snow, the budding trees, the warm breezes. They were all signs of the new spring; signs of new life and hope after the long bitter winter season.

For Shanawdithit it was now more than a little bitter sweet. It was a relief that the cold harsh winter was once more behind them, but with only fifteen of them left, there was little room to feel any kind of hope. Constant harassment by the settlers, no safe access to the sea coast, and illness had all conspired to bring them to the point of no return. Just as her uncle Nonosabasut had feared, the Beothuk were disappearing. She knew she was probably one of the last of her nation. There were days when she wondered how she had made it this far; why she had been spared when so many of her family had been taken from her. It seemed tragedy and sadness were all she had known during her twenty three years.

Her uncle Jaywritt and her cousin Aaduth had left for the coast a little over a month ago. They had decided to hunt the monau that would be floating on the ice pans drifting past the island this time of year. It was a good opportunity to get fresh meat and oil, as well as new skins to make clothing. With more Buggishaman settling on the coast each year it was risky, but the tribe had nothing left to eat so Jaywritt had felt it was a necessary risk that had to be taken. She remembered listening in the dark as Doodlebewshet had begged them not to go the night before they left. She wondered then if she would ever see them again.

With more than a month gone by and no sign of them, the remaining tribe members feared the worst.

Shanawdithit looked across the fire at Doodlebewshet and her daughter. Both had been coughing uncontrollably through the night and most of the day. Tears moistened the corners of her eyes. These were her closest family now, in fact they were the only family she had. They had adopted her when she lost her mother and father, and had treated her as a sister and a daughter.

The bony claw of fear now gripped her heart and squeezed. She knew they had the dreaded disease the Buggishaman called consumption. There was nothing she could do to help them. She had tried everything she knew. There was no food left in storage, and they were starving. She had not inherited the hunting skills of her parents, and had never mastered the hathemay. Since the day she lost Preduc on the ice she had no appetite for hunting anyway.

Without Jaywritt and Aaduth, there was no one left to hunt for the family.

A black cloud of despair filled the wigwam. There didn't seem to be any air left to breathe. *I've got to do something* she thought in a panic. *I've got to fight this! There has to be something we can do.*

"Let us go to the coast," she blurted out. At first she hadn't realized she had spoken aloud as she fought her way back to reality. "There will be shell fish and birds eggs there. We will be able to find something to eat," she continued. Her breathing seemed to be getting easier as she spoke. The moment was passing.

"There are also Buggishaman," replied Doodlebewshet, with faint stirrings of alarm in her voice. She bent over as she was overcome with another fit of violent coughing.

"There is nothing left for us here at this camp," argued Shanawdithit. She had noticed the traces of blood on Doodlebewshet's hands as she took them away from her face. There were also traces at the corners of her mouth.

"It will take us at least a week to get there. She is not well enough. Look at her," she inclined her head in the direction of her daughter, Linguitt, who was curled in a ball, sleeping restlessly nearby.

"We have to try Doodlebewshet. You know if we stay here we will die anyway," Shanawdithit persisted.

"Is it not better to die in our own home than at the hand of the Buggishaman?"

Shanawdithit did not reply immediately. She concentrated on the odemet she was rubbing into the skin of her bare legs. She knew they had to leave here, and soon, she thought, as Doodlebewshet's body was wracked with another fit of coughing.

"The sooner we leave the better," she said. "If we put it off much longer, you are going to be too sick to walk all that way."

"Stop pushing me," croaked Doodlebewshet between coughs. "I'll decide in the morning." She pulled the blanket up around her shoulders and stretched out next to her sleeping daughter in an act of dismissal.

Shanawdithit realized the conversation was over, and she would get nothing further from her tonight. She busied herself with coating the rest of her body with a fresh coat of odemet mixed with animal fat. She had to keep busy and not let those dark thoughts return.

Before falling asleep, she picked up a burned stick that had fallen out of the fire. When she was sure it was cool enough, she began drawing on the piece of birch rind that was sitting in her lap. Drawing was like a medicine. It helped distract her from the hopelessness of their situation.

Her eyes moved around the room to the sketches hanging on the walls. She would have to leave most of them if they left in a day or so. Those drawings were her connection to her past and to her family who were no longer with her. Drawing had helped her get through the worst of the pain. It had helped keep them close to her. The drawings were all that she had left.

Her eyes returned to the large piece of birch rind in her lap. In the faint light provided by the flickering fire, she bent over the birch and began to draw the fifteen who were left.

Her eyes hurt.

Squinting against the bright light, she opened her eyes enough to find the source. Lifting herself up on one elbow she discovered the door flap was partially open. A stream of bright sunlight had found its way through the small opening and onto her face, gently forcing her awake.

She wished the sun hadn't awakened her. She was having such a good dream. All of her family was there in the dream. She couldn't remember it all. The details were foggy and just at the edge of her memory but she remembered there was laughter and everyone was happy.

She became aware of a dull ache in her back. It must be from the awkward position she had slept in. From the unfinished drawing on the ground and the piece of charcoal still clutched in her fingers, it was obvious she had fallen asleep while still working on the sketch. She gingerly opened and closed her cramped fingers until the tingling stopped. Slowly she pushed to her feet.

Linguitt was still sleeping near the fire, but Doodlebewshet was not there. She was outside somewhere. Shanawdithit could hear her coughing as she moved around the clearing.

Bending low, she stepped through the door into the warm sunlight. Doodlebewshet was talking with Laddiwett, the oldest women of the tribe. The first thing Shanawdithit noticed was that Laddiwett was standing some distance away from Doodlebewshet, as if she was afraid to get too close to her. As she drew near the two women, she could hear the conversation, and what she heard made her heart sink.

The old woman looked her way and said, "You have to take them from here, Shanawdithit. If you stay, we will all get the sickness. There are not enough of us left to survive this. It will kill us all."

Miserably, Doodlebewshet replied, "Where will we go? There is nowhere left for us."

Shanawdithit felt as though she had been punched in the stomach. The fact that Laddiwett was right didn't make it any easier. They were being forced to leave. Most likely they would never see these people again. She did not want it to end this way.

Shanawdithit took Doodlebewshet by the arm and helped her stand up from the tree stump she had been sitting on.

"She is right, Doodlebewshet, we have to leave to protect the rest of the tribe." Over Doodlebewshet's shoulder she met the other women's sad eyes, and nodded in acknowledgement of her pain. Holding her arm to support her, she led Doodlebewshet back to their wigwam.

Once inside, Doodlebewshet brushed her arm away and busied herself with selecting the few things they could carry with them. Even though she tried to keep her face averted, Shanawdithit saw the tears on her cheek, and swallowed hard around the bitter lump in her own throat. She knew it was the right thing to do, but she knew Doodlebewshet was thinking as she was, that they would never see any of the tribe again. This would be goodbye.

She helped Linguitt gather some clothes together and then helped her put on an extra layer to keep her warm. Then she selected the drawing she had been working on last night and slipped it, along with the charcoal, into her bag. Sadly she looked around at what had been their home for the last few years. She knew the tribe would burn it as soon as they left. It was the only way they knew to protect themselves from the sickness.

Shanawdithit glanced up at the sky as she held the flap aside for the other two to step outside Overhead the sun was now obscured by heavy gray clouds. The bright sunlight that she had awakened to was washed away and the day had transformed itself to match the dark and heavy spirits of the camp. All of the other ten tribe members had gathered in the clearing to watch them go. Their subdued goodbyes were smothered in a heavy blanket of sadness, made worse by the necessary lack of contact.

"If Jaywritt and Aaduth return, tell them we are gone to the coast," Doodlebewshet said to the little group. "Tell them to come and find us there."

Then she turned, gripped Linguitt and Shanawdithit's hands, and the three women walked into the waiting forest that quickly swallowed them up from view as if they had never been there.

The End

Author's Notes

History tells us the three Beothuk women made it to safety, surrendering to a settler by the name of William Cull who lived near Exploits Island in Notre Dame Bay. Although Shanawdithit lived for another six years and provided us, through her drawings and descriptions, most of what little we know of the ill-fated Beothuks, the other two women died of tuberculosis (consumption) within days of their capture/surrender.

When Shanawdithit succumbed to the same disease, on June 6, 1829, she earned the undesirable label of "the last known Beothuk". The fate of the twelve who remained in the interior when Shanawdithit was "taken" is unknown and has undoubtedly been a subject of discussion and conjecture around the kitchen table of many Newfoundlanders over the years.

Many of us would just as soon forget our ancestor's role in this troubling time in the history of our beautiful island, but nevertheless, it is an important, albeit shameful, piece of who we are. The settlers' approach was not all that different than that taken in many other places in the New World with respect to the treatment of native peoples. What makes the Newfoundland story unique is the end result. The Beothuk, unlike so many other native groups, did not survive.

Unfortunately, very little tangible evidence remains to remind us of the passing of the Beothuk nation.

In 1927 the Exploits River was dammed, raising the level of water in the Red Indian Lake by approximately fifteen feet, effectively burying most of their campsites underwater.

Shanawdithit's burial site, at the Parish Church of St. Mary the Virgin on the south side of St. John's harbor, was lost to make way for the railway in the early 1900s'.

The plaque acknowledging the location of her burial site was later removed to make way for the new sewage processing plant at the west end of the St. John's harbor.

All this in the name of progress!

Although this is primarily a work of fiction, the characters, events and times have been built around the scanty recorded history of the Beothuk.

I believe, as time goes by, we are in danger of losing this story and thus the plight of this gentle, proud nation will fade into the shadows of our memories. My objective in writing this book is to refresh our memories as Newfoundlanders, and to help preserve, if at all possible, this piece of our vibrant history. We are fast approaching the 200th anniversary of the death of Shanawdithit and it is important that our children meet the Beothuks.

If you have just finished reading this book, you have been introduced to Shanawdithit and her family. All I ask is that you introduce them to your friends and family. If, like some people (who I'll never understand) you came to read this last page first, then I encourage you to go back and start at the beginning. You are about to meet a great family who I hope you carry in your memory from this day forward.

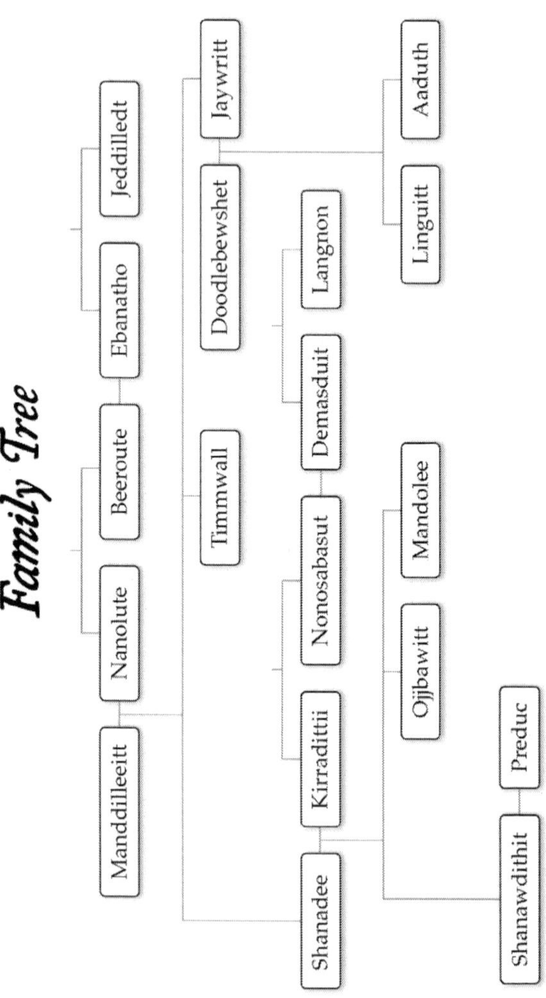
Family Tree
Manddilleeitt
Nanolute
Beeroute
Ebanatho
Jeddilledt
Timmwall
Doodlebewshet
Jaywritt
Shanadee
Kirradittii
Nonosabasut
Demasduit
Langnon
Ojjbawitt
Mandolee
Linguitt
Aaduth
Shanawdithit
Preduc

Glossary of Terms

The following represents a list of Beothuk words used in this book. These were provided to William Cormack by Shanawdithit, during their many conversations.

Beothuk words

Buggishaman	*white man*
Gossett	*land of the dead*
Hathemay	*bow*
Moisamadrook	*wolf*
Monau	*seal*
Odemet	*red ochre*
Tapaithook	*canoe*
Wasemook	*salmon*

Locations

The Great Lake	*Red Indian Lake*
The Great River	*Exploits River*

Historical Characters

A number of historical characters are represented in this book. As a work of historical fiction, fictional characters are used to develop the stories of the historical characters.

Resources

A History and Ethnography of the Beothuk

Ingeborg Marshall – McGill-Queen's University Press 1996

The Book of Newfoundland-Volume III

The First Newfoundlanders: The Beothucks

James R. Thoms

Lecture on the Aborigines of Newfoundland

Joseph Noad

Report of Mr. W. E. Cormack's journey in search of the Red Indians in Newfoundland

William E. Cormack

Other Books by the Author

Watch for Terry's second book in this series, *"Red Indian – The Final Days."*

In 1823 Shanawdithit and her two companions walked out of the woods and surrendered to William Cull, leaving behind twelve tribe members…..all that remained of the Beothuk nation. This book will tell their stories.

For information on how to obtain books;

www.terryfoss.ca

terryfoss@nf.sympatico.ca

Printed in Great Britain
by Amazon.co.uk, Ltd.,
Marston Gate.